PRAISE FOR

THIN SPACE

"Sometimes you need a book that hurts so good, and Jody Casella's powerful, authentically told debut is one of those books. *Thin Space* carries you through the heart of what it means to love and lose, to regret and move forward . . . and won't set you down until long after its riveting finale."

JENNIFER CASTLE, author of
Beginning of After and *You Look Different in Real Life*

"An eerie yet ultimately hopeful exploration of grief, guilt, friendship and redemption, *Thin Space* captivated me from start to finish."

Colleen Clayton, author of *What Happens Next*

"Take off your shoes and prepare to stroll barefoot through a novel richly grounded in love, loss, and the redemptive power of truth. But don't get too comfortable, because the twist at the end will knock your socks off."

Mike Mullin, author of *Ashfall*

THIN
SPACE

JODY CASELLA

SIMON PULSE
New York London Toronto Sydney New Delhi

BEYOND WORDS
Hillsboro, Oregon

SIMON PULSE

BEYOND WORDS

An imprint of Simon & Schuster
Children's Publishing Division
1230 Avenue of the Americas
New York, NY 10020

20827 N.W. Cornell Road, Suite 500
Hillsboro, Oregon 97124-9808
503-531-8700 / 503-531-8773 fax
www.beyondword.com

First Beyond Words/Simon Pulse edition September 2013
Copyright © 2013 by Jody Casella

SIMON PULSE is a trademark of Simon & Schuster, Inc., and related logo is a registered trademark of Simon & Schuster, Inc.
Beyond Words is an imprint of Simon & Schuster, Inc. and the Beyond Words logo is a registered trademark of Beyond Words Publishing, Inc.

For information about special discounts for bulk purchases,
please contact Simon & Schuster Special Sales at 1-866-506-1949 or
business@simonandschuster.com.

The Simon & Schuster Speakers Bureau can bring authors to your live event. For more information or to book an event contact the Simon & Schuster Speakers Bureau at 1-866-248-3049 or visit our website at www.simonspeakers.com.

Interior design: Sara E. Blum
The text of this book was set in Adobe Garamond Pro and Interstate.

Manufactured in the United States of America

10 9 8 7 6 5 4 3 2

Library of Congress Cataloging-in-Publication Data

Casella, Jody.
   Thin space / Jody Casella. — Beyond Words/Simon Pulse edition.
      pages   cm
   Summary: Consumed by guilt and secrets about his twin brother's death, Marsh
      Windsor is looking for a thin space—a place where the barrier between this world
      and the next is thin enough for a person to cross over—in hopes of setting things
      right.
   [1. Supernatural—Fiction. 2. Conduct of life—Fiction. 3. Interpersonal relations
      Fiction. 4. Brothers—Fiction. 5. Twins—Fiction. 6. High schools—Fiction.
      7. Schools—Fiction. 8. Dead—Fiction.]   I. Title.
   PZ7.C26772Thi 2014
   [Fic]—dc23
                                                                    2012045691
ISBN 978-1-58270-435-7 (hc)
ISBN 978-1-58270-392-3 (pbk)
ISBN 978-1-4424-6814-6 (eBook)

FOR

RICK, BEN, AND JANE ESKILDSEN

All foot covering must be removed. This practice is a requirement for successful entry and not merely a symbolic gesture of humility upon approaching a sacred space.

Stones or rocks serve as an indication of the border between this world and the Other. Additionally, the stones themselves may hold magical properties. (No doubt you have heard of the Spirit said to reside in all manner of natural and inanimate objects.)

Even scholars debate about that moment when the soul enters the body, the common notion being when the mother feels the first stirrings of life in her womb. The soul's departure (death)—if such event should occur in the same physical space—creates a permanent fissure in the boundary.

As to the nature of the environment, the personal accounts are similar in describing a cold, mist-like substance. Reports one observer: "It was like the air itself had turned to liquid ice. And long after I returned, I could still sense the creep of it in my very bones."

Curious Accounts of the Thin Space
Edited by Sir Geoffrey Davis
Published 1848 in London by Harvey, Mavor & Jones, Inc.

Prologue
Three Months Ago

"Marsh."

The light was bright. Glaring. I tried to turn my head, but a sharp tug locked me in place. Ugh! Something was clamped between my lips. It snaked down my throat, so I couldn't breathe. I jerked my hands, wanting to claw whatever the hell it was away, but someone's fingers curled around mine and held them down.

"It's okay," a voice said. "You're okay, Marsh."

"What?" But I could only grunt the word.

I forgot I couldn't move my head, and I tried to turn again. Which freaking hurt. I couldn't see anything but light. It seared my eyes so I shut them, but the light kept burning. I remembered light blazing like that . . . headlights . . . looming brighter, closer. My hands twitched and I felt my fingers still clamped around the steering wheel. Felt my feet pounding at the brakes. Saw him next to me—his mouth open, his eyes wide—as the light sliced his face.

A different voice said, "Marsh?"

I forgot I couldn't talk, but I tried. "Guh?" I said. That hurt too. Everything hurt. My leg throbbed. My chest ached like some 250-pound defensive tackle had just slammed into it. But my head—God. The pain shot from the center of my skull and somehow also tunneled in from the outside—one all-encompassing, pulsating wound. Maybe *I* hit the windshield too?

His face was a slow-motion series of snapshots: Pissed off. Confused. Scared—

And just like that, I knew. Two seconds earlier I'd thought I was in pain. But that pain was nothing. Nothing. Because now I knew.

My brother was dead.

1
Now

Every morning, I walk by Mrs. Hansel's house and plan my break-in.

Today I think about kicking down doors, shattering windows. I have a one-second flash of myself climbing down the chimney. Which just shows how far gone I am lately.

I stop at the foot of the driveway and squint at the two lines of concrete that lead back to the unattached garage. A realtor was out here not too long ago, mowing the stubble of grass that runs down the center, clipping the bushes, yanking dead flowers out of the flowerbeds. I wonder if she forgot to lock up.

The house has a basement with an outside entrance. It's where Mrs. Hansel kept her hedge trimmers. I'm thinking maybe I can sneak inside there, slip down the stairs before anyone sees me. Once, my brother and I broke into our own house that way. His idea. *No way am I going to stand out here in the cold,* he said. *Dad'll get over it.* Big grin and he was already stomping his boot against the latch.

Before I can lose my nerve, I sprint toward the backyard, keeping in the shadows along the side of the house. The basement doors jut out from the ground like a storm cellar. When I give them a tug, they don't budge. Without thinking, I kick the metal handles.

Shit! I have to grit my teeth to keep from yelling. I hop around on one foot, holding the throbbing one in my hands. I can't deal with another injury right now. Shattered leg. Split forehead and chin. Bashed up nose. I've had enough battered body parts. But I instantly regret the thought. I'm the one left alive. Who the hell am I to feel sorry for myself? Anyway, my stupid foot isn't broken.

The school bus rumbles around the corner and I hobble back up the driveway, and then half stagger down the street toward my stop. Big shocker, Lindsay and Heather are standing there yakking it up. "Hey, Marsh," they drone in the same nasally tone.

I ignore them and tramp up the grooved bus steps, slick and cold under my bare feet. I plunk down in my usual seat, one foot still pulsing from that kick at the door handle.

Why am I such an idiot?

The bus jerks forward and we're almost past Mrs. Hansel's. I blink at the for sale sign in the front yard and wonder when they'll be holding another open house.

They had one a few weeks ago, and I marched up the walk like I knew what I was doing—didn't even ring the doorbell. You don't have to during an open house. I strode right into the front room and made it halfway across, halfway toward the place where the hospice people had set up the bed.

The floor slants in that house, sloping down from the entryway over to the fireplace. I raised my bare foot, thinking that the floor slanted right where I wanted to go, like the house was leading me to the spot. For just a second, the bed was there again, the white blankets spilling over, Mrs. Hansel propped up, her thin body sinking into the pillows. I could see her bony finger shaking. *I can make a thin space,* she said. *You'll see. There's going to be a thin space right here in this room.*

But just as I was about to put my foot down, the realtor came around the corner from the dining room. I must've been grinning like a doofball because I could picture it, being whisked away. One second swaying on the tilted floorboards, the next second gone. Well, that would scare the living crap out of the realtor, to see me sucked out of the room.

Now, just thinking about how I blew my chance ticks me off all over again. I should've shoved past that lady and kept going, stepped in, pressed down—

The bus jolts to a stop in front of the school and I have to brace myself to face another day here. Remind myself why I'm doing it. What the point is.

This morning, it's searching the gym. I'm covering the place diagonally today because it hits me that the up and down pattern I've been doing might've led me to miss some spots.

As far as thin spaces go, the gym has strong possibilities. You hear about it on the news: Kid passes out after a basketball game. A hidden heart problem. Never heard of it happening at Andover High, but hey, it could've. The school is old. My grandparents went here. Mrs. Hansel did too, now that I think about it. Occasionally women have strolled around here pregnant—which is the key detail and the thing that makes finding a thin space so freaking hard.

When Mrs. Hansel first told us about it, my brother and me, that was the sticking point. Or really, that was the part my brother kept circling back to. Last spring when Mrs. Hansel was just the weird old lady who lived down the street. We were only helping her to get our school-required service hours. Mow her lawn. Lug boxes out of the attic. And the whole time she was blathering about thin spaces.

They're like doorways, according to Google, places where the wall between this world and the next one is thinner. Where the dead can come back. And where living people can enter the world of the dead.

But here's the thing you can't google: How to *make* a thin space. Mrs. Hansel told us it all came down to your soul leaving your body in the same spot it came through. That's what makes a place thinner. She had it stuck in her head that her point of entry was the front room of her house, so that's where she planned to die.

My brother had jumped all over that. *You were born in this room?* he'd asked. But Mrs. Hansel had just smiled. No. She wasn't talking about *birth*. She was talking about *souls*. "Quickening" they used to call it, when a pregnant woman first feels a child move in her body. Then she and my brother went off onto some ethical tangent about when life begins, and I quit listening.

Which is too bad. Because now it'd be nice to know a few more details.

I'm finished with my slide through the gym. The diagonal method, big surprise, got me nowhere. Slim-to-none chance that a soul came through in the boys' locker room, but I weave my way around the whole place just in case. I head into the shower area where my feet slap tiles, still wet from morning showers. The football team must've just finished their AM workouts.

Last year around this time my brother and I were down here every morning. We had to ride our bikes to school in the dark. I always griped about it, but he'd just laugh at me, tell me to quit whining, and call me "little brother," our private joke, since he was really only three minutes older.

But I don't want to think about last year. I push out of the gym and trudge down the hall, walking the wall's edge. Apparently, no one ever left the world leaning against a school wall. No one ever died standing in front of my locker either, but for the hell of it, I open the door and stick my foot inside. Even as my skin hits the metal bottom, I think, *Jeez, is it possible that someone could die* inside *a locker?* I whirl my head around, considering. If there's even a small chance, I'm in trouble. I'll have to poke my foot into, what? Eighteen hundred lockers? Not counting the half-size ones in the gym.

I almost laugh. Even if someone did die in a locker, no way that same soul came into the world there. I can't imagine a pregnant woman, even the rare pregnant girl around here, stuffing her stomach into a locker.

I pull my foot out and shuffle to class.

Morning's a haze, and then somehow, it's lunchtime. Of course I've already slid my feet all over the cafeteria.

The food's so crappy that I'd been hoping someone over the years would've succumbed to it. Choked on it. Been poisoned by it.

No such luck.

Whatever. I plunk down at the end of the theater-people table and dump out the contents of my lunch bag. Well-balanced as always, thanks Mom! PB and J on whole wheat. An apple. Bag of baked chips. While I eat, I rub my feet back and forth across the grimy floor squares.

Because here's what I'm thinking: Let's say someone, a pregnant school secretary hypothetically speaking, once walked through this cafeteria. Crossed the floor, rubbing her stomach, eyeing the snack machine, and then she feels it: a twitch, the first kick of her baby. Flash forward sixteen years to that same kid. A theater buff, we'll call him. The kid sitting right now at the other end of the table, about to crunch into a Cheeto. So here's my twisted thought: maybe he has a fatal allergic reaction to overly processed food. He flings himself backward right there, right on that exact spot where his mother, the school secretary, once stood.

I bite into my apple, eyeing the Cheeto kid, who, although kind of pale in his black turtleneck, doesn't seem to be on the verge of leaving our world any time soon. Plus, now that I think about it, he's not from here. He's one of the few people who moved to Andover later. Third grade was when that guy first showed up in our perfect town.

"Marsh."

Wishful thinking, I tell myself. There's no thin space in the cafeteria. There's no thin space in the whole damn school.

It's in Mrs. Hansel's house, and I'm going to have to get back in there if—

"Marsh."

I snap my head up and squint, confused for a second by the hulking guy swaying over me. Chuck Gardner. Long-lost football buddy. Old sparring partner on the field.

"Hey, you can hardly see that scar on your face anymore," he says. "Uh, so, uh, I was wondering if you wanted to— well, some of us are going out after the game tonight and . . ."

It's Friday?

He plows on, not looking at me, his eyes fixed somewhere over my head. A part of me wants to help him, throw him a bone for making the effort. Not many people bother anymore.

"Nothing big. Just some of the guys, like before when we . . ."

But another part of me wonders if I should stop him, point out the obvious: *Look, Chuck, our friendship, like everything else these days, is over.*

He glances over his shoulder and I can't help it. I follow that glance, all the way over to the snack machine, where the football players sprawl out watching this potentially dramatic scene. Without planning to, I scan the football groupie table where the girls I used to know (*Kate, Logan, I refuse to acknowledge you*) are pretending not to stare.

I seem to catch every eye as I pivot my head. Even the damn theater people have stopped talking. Pale, turtleneck, Cheeto guy doesn't even bother to pretend. He's blatantly gaping at me.

I imagine him clutching his head, gasping for air. One of those ticking time bombs you hear about, walking around with a brain aneurysm and one day the vein or artery or whatever bursts right here in the cafeteria. In the same place where his pregnant mother once walked.

And sick as it is, all I can think about is how freaking awesome that would be. If there were a thin space right here, and I dropped my foot down and got pulled into it, like a vortex, jerking me out of my seat. Leaving behind my nutritious lunch scraps and the staring people and the—

"Marsh?"

I blink at Chuck, who I'm surprised to note is still swaying over me. My hand is gripped around my apple so tightly that my knuckles are white. For a wild moment I consider throwing it at him, imagine the fruit bouncing off his forehead. It might wake him up. Get him to really look at me.

I shake my head a few seconds before opening my mouth. "I'm busy tonight," I say. And I'm a little surprised at how my voice sounds as I croak out the words.

"Busy," Chuck repeats.

I nod. *That's right. I'm busy looking for a way out of this world, okay, buddy?*

But I don't say that, of course, and then, thank God, the bell rings. I stand up, hurl my apple in the trashcan, and push past Chuck, sliding my feet the whole way along the dirty floor until I'm out of there.

2
Breaking and Entering

Saturday I take the city bus over to the hospital. I've got one hand around a bunch of cheap flowers I picked up in the gift shop, so I can look like I belong around here as I shuffle down hallways.

My brother was the one who brought up the idea, now that I think about it. Back when we were humoring Mrs. Hansel about thin spaces. *Cemeteries, funeral homes . . .* He ticked the possibilities off on his fingers. *And hey!* He eyed me, smirking. *How about hospitals?*

I don't know about cemeteries and funeral homes. But hospitals? What other place would have such a good shot of containing one? Souls check out of this miserable world every day in a hospital. And souls definitely check in here. The same souls, though?

That's the catch. When is it *exactly* that a soul comes through? I'm sure as hell hoping it isn't at conception. That would really make my search harder. Somehow I don't think many people are conceived in a freaking hospital. Which leaves somewhere along the way in the pregnancy process.

A few obviously expecting women pass by me. Maybe they're on the way to some birthing class. Who knows? But this hallway seems a good place to start.

For the moment, the area is deserted. I drag my feet across the floor, trying to ignore the antiseptic smell that permeates this whole place. The noxious odor shoots me right back to the days after the accident. Even through my busted nose, I could smell it.

Apparently, I'd been out of it for a few days. When I woke up, my mother and father were standing by my bed sobbing. I tried to touch my face but the IV cord tugged my arm back. Probably a good thing. Later, when I finally got a good look, after I begged the nurse to hold up a mirror, I could see the problem. The face that looked back at me was not mine.

The intercom clicks on. Some doctor needed in OR stat. I reach the corner and turn, dragging my feet down the center of the hallway now. At least they keep these floors fairly clean. I don't feel much dust. Or maybe the skin on my feet has toughened up.

I hear talking, footsteps. I take a step out of the way as several people turn the corner. When they pass, I slide back to where I left off. I do this all day, peeking my head into rooms, pacing around the few that are unoccupied.

Around four o'clock I give up, head over to an elevator. Could the elevator contain a thin space? Who the hell knows?

Since no one else gets on with me, I skim the floor as I jab the button. Feel the whoosh as the bottom drops out.

Unfortunately, I don't get whisked out of this world.

Outside I catch the city bus. Ignore the passengers' stares. When I first started going barefoot, it ticked me off. I mean, who cares if I'm not wearing shoes? It's not like there's some law. Okay, maybe there are guidelines. Health codes. But isn't that *my* problem? Broken glass, germs, cold weather—if I can deal with these irritations, what difference does it make to anyone else?

Whatever. I can handle stares. Funny thing: for a while, I thought I would need to come up with some kind of story. But not one person asked me about my feet. It was like some unspoken agreement, like someone had fired off a mass email. I'd notice people look down, and then avert their eyes. After a couple weeks, they didn't even bother to look down. Probably a good thing, since my reasoning sounds nuts.

The bus spits me out in downtown Andover and I trudge up the road, stuff my hands in my pockets. It's getting colder lately. The sun's just a memory. But that's how it is in November, beginning of "cloud season," as people in Andover like to call it. Every day, the sky stretches out gray.

I cross the street so I won't have to walk in front of the movie theater. I hate that place. It reminds me of the double date from hell—Logan and Kate, giggling, hanging all over us. And him—him! My brother—looking right at me when he kissed her. But I don't want to think about that.

Leave the movie theater behind. Turn the corner and I'm striding up my street. Fairly certain there are no thin spaces on this stretch of sidewalk, but I carefully smack my feet down anyway. When I near Mrs. Hansel's house, I've got what's probably an insane thought about smashing one of the basement windows around back. It might be big enough for me to squeeze through, and because of the landscaping, I'm pretty sure no one will see what I'm doing.

I glance around quickly. No nosy neighbors lurking, so I scuffle down the driveway, kneel, shove the bushes out of the way. I must be losing my mind. There's no way I can fit through that window. And I'm not even the bulked-up guy I was before the accident.

I fall back on my heels, let out a sigh. My eyes settle on the basement doors. It makes my foot ache just remembering how I kicked them yesterday morning. I don't know what makes me do it, but I stand up, waltz over, and tug at the handle.

One door swings open.

Huh. For a second, my heart seems to stop beating. I feel it start up again, thudding in my throat as I practically throw myself down the stairs. I stop, reach up to shut the door. Then it's pitch black and I'm blinking in the dark, trying to get my bearings.

There's a hanging switch somewhere—at least I think I remember one from times my brother and I were working down here, hauling stuff in and out. I lurch forward, flailing my hands, feeling for the chain. When I do, I give it a yank. Nothing.

I start laughing. I can't help it. It was one of *his* jobs back in the spring to change the light bulbs for Mrs. Hansel.

"Hey," I say into the blackness. "You must've missed one." Hearing my own voice, even wild and shrill as it is, makes me feel halfway better, strips away some of my hysteria. Because I can imagine him answering. Like it's just another long Saturday slaving away for Mrs. Hansel, and if I yell loud enough, he'll hear me, poke his head down here, flick the damn light on.

"I'm coming," I call, and my heart jackhammers as I stagger across the floor in what I hope is the direction of the stairs. When I get there, I'll feel my way up the steps, let myself into the kitchen. Only a few strides and I can be in the front room. Step into the thin space. Get the hell out of here and find him. See him. Do what I've got to do.

My fingers hit a cobweb, and I shudder. "I'm coming," I yell again.

Now I imagine he's the one laughing. He didn't believe her. He thought she was crazy. Really, we both did. "Blah blah thin space" was what it sounded like to us then. Who would've blamed us? All those creepy stories from "the old country," as she called it—

My hip whacks something. *Ow.* I grope around and find I've bumped into the stair rail. I try to slow my breathing, keep my feet steady as I climb. I can't mess this up again. *Focus*, I tell myself. *One step at a time. Just get to the top, open the door, and then run toward it.*

There. I've found the knob. I grip it with a shaking hand. The damn thing is locked. I try it again, not wanting to believe it.

My mind's spinning. I lean my head on the door. Try the knob again. *Break it down,* is what I'm thinking. *Just kick the door in.* Who cares? Once I'm inside, I'm going to disappear anyway. Someone else will have to worry about the consequences.

But just as I'm about to heave my body against the wood, I hear footsteps clomping across the floor. A click, and then a slit of light leaks under the door. I can just make out my clenched hand.

"My goodness!" The familiar voice is bright. "Has the house sold already?" It's Mrs. Golden. Self-proclaimed neighborhood watch captain. President of the welcoming committee. Coincidentally, she's also my school guidance counselor. Great. I squeeze the doorknob so I won't be tempted to punch the wall.

"I know." Another voice. Which has got to belong to the realtor. "Not even two months. And in this market!"

"My goodness," Mrs. Golden says again. "Can't imagine anyone living in this house but Rosie Hansel. She grew up in this house, you know. Lived here her whole life. Died in this house."

"I heard about that. I'm so sorry." But the realtor doesn't really sound it. "We don't have to share that piece of information with—"

"Oh my! I wouldn't dream of it."

"Buyers are a nice family. They're moving in this weekend. Single mom. Two teenagers."

"Hmm. I think I just processed those transfer files at school. A boy and a girl . . ."

They keep blathering on. I'm clutching the doorknob so hard it's probably imprinting onto my hand. *I'm going to wait it out,* is what I'm thinking. *I'll stand here all day if I have to.*

"Darn it!" I hear the realtor say. And I'm horrified to feel a jiggling movement on the doorknob. "Do you happen to know which key opens the basement door?"

And then I'm tripping down the stairs like a maniac. That slit of light keeps the place from being completely black, but I can still barely see, and I can hear the clatter of keys, a clicking sound, and the door opening as I huff it toward my exit.

"You seem to know so much about this house," the realtor is saying. "Do you know where the light switch is?"

And Mrs. Golden's voice. "On the wall, by the door."

I've reached the back steps when the light switches on. The room blazes up, and I thank God, because I realize I was just about to trip over a bucket of pebbles. It's on the second step, and I leap over it, heave open one of the metal doors, throw myself into the yard, and then as carefully as possible in my state of total mania, I close the door.

My heart's slamming in my chest as I race across the backyards. Bucket of pebbles! Jeez.

Ironic too, since I'm the one who put them there last spring, when Mrs. Hansel had us doing odd jobs. And somehow that meant collecting these stones so she could scatter them all over the place. On the tops of doorframes. In random piles in the corners of rooms.

She was figuring out borders, marking her potential thin space. I know that now. But then, my brother and I rolled our eyes.

She's out of her mind. I hear his voice plain as day. *You know that, right?*

No. No. No. The word pounds in my head. *She wasn't crazy. Couldn't be crazy. Because there* has *to be a thin space. Because I have to go into it.* I sail over a hedge, trip over a tree root, pinball away from the trunk.

I can almost hear his snickering.

Listen, I imagine myself telling him. *You weren't there. You didn't see her that last day. When she was in the bed in the front room. When she pointed her finger. She stared right at me. She knew— She said—*

Oh, little brother. He shakes his head, smirks, and I want to smack him.

For two seconds I'm pissed off, and it's such a relief from this panic and the sickening ache that never freaking goes away. But then it all slams back into me and now it's wrapped up in a nice slab of guilt.

Like I have a right to be pissed off at anyone. Like I have a right to even *be* here.

I'm sprinting up the back steps into my house before it hits me that once again I was so close to that front room, and once again I've blown my shot. And then I remember what the realtor said about the new family moving in. My stomach seizes and I have to clutch at it to keep from hurling all over my kitchen.

How am I going to break in now? How am I going to get into the thin space and fix this mess?

3
Stranger at the Bus Stop

Monday morning it's weird to see lights on in Mrs. Hansel's house. But I have to remind myself it's not her house anymore.

Yesterday I itched to go outside, stride right by Mrs. Golden and her crew of cronies who milled around at the curb and chatted it up with the moving men. What stopped me from doing it? Why would I care what those busybodies thought? The front door was propped open, for God's sake!

Because you're a coward, says a voice that sounds suspiciously like my brother's. I laugh into my hands, but it's like I'm choking. I realize I'm standing in front of Mrs. Hansel's house, rocking back and forth on cold feet, staring at the place like some kind of stalker.

I get a flash of Mrs. Hansel one of those Saturday mornings, waving a list: Clean out the closets. Box up old clothes . . . Her kids were going to come, she said, to get the stuff they wanted. She went on about it while my brother and I worked. About her kids. Her dead husband. About growing up in that house and Andover over the years. Blah blah blah.

I can't remember exactly when she started telling us about thin spaces.

I trudge down the sidewalk. Someone's at the corner waiting. I don't think it's Lindsay or Heather. As I get closer, the first thing I can pick out in the murky light is a ponytail. The girl's back is to me. I don't want to scare her, so I clear my throat.

She turns and her breath eddies in front of her face. She's very pink cheeked. I do a quick scan. Note the blond hair pulled back, a jacket clearly not warm enough for Andover, jeans—those flashy designer ones—and boots. Same plush boots that Kate and Logan wear. It figures.

She's scanning me too. I see her eyes widen when she takes in my bare feet, then they readjust and her mouth curves into a shaky smile.

I clear my throat again. "Your family moved into that gray house?"

She nods.

But Lindsay and Heather are suddenly upon us. "Marsh," they say. I notice them checking out the new girl. They don't bother hiding their appraisal. Lindsay even moves her head up and down like she's making some kind of mental checklist. New Girl will probably pass their inspection. She's wearing the approved Andover female attire. She's got the ponytail. She's cute enough, if I cared to think about it.

If she does meet their criteria, though, Lindsay and Heather don't clue her in on it. Instead, they blow her off, jumping into one of their inane conversations.

"Then I was like get out of my face."

"You did NOT say that."

"Uh, yeah I did."

New Girl shoots a look in my direction. Her cheeks are really pink. She's got to be freezing. Her jacket is worthless. But maybe she doesn't care. I'll be the first person to admit that I don't understand girls.

The bus squeaks up, and Lindsay and Heather march between New Girl and me like we aren't even there. New Girl doesn't budge. She's got a funny expression on her face when she looks past where I'm standing to Mrs. Hansel's house—*her* house now. She takes a step in that direction, and I bet I know what she's thinking. She wants to run back home, forget the damn bus and the new school she's got to go to, forget the idiotic girls and the crazy barefoot guy, and just get the hell out of here.

So we've got that in common. One side of my mouth twitches up. I hold my arm out, think the words *after you*, and New Girl sighs out a swirl of mist and climbs onto the bus.

I don't run into her again until lunch.

I'm sitting in the corner today, over where the lunch line exits. The table's wedged against a brick column and gives me a nice, unobstructed view of the people spilling out of the doorway with their trays. It's as good a place as any for someone to drop dead.

I'm hunched over, just about to chow down on my tuna on whole wheat when I see her. She's paused in the doorway, the lunch tray shaking in her hands.

Several weird thoughts flip through my mind. One, those pink cheeks. It hits me that it's got to be makeup and not some natural freshness. Which makes me think of Kate and Logan, and I can't help shooting a glance in the direction of the football groupie table but neither of them are there, and who cares. Second thought: New Girl's clearly nervous and doesn't know anyone, so why can't I be the one to show her the ropes around here and she'll be so thankful she'll invite me in . . .

I roll my apple between my hands. This could be my ticket back into Mrs. Hansel's house. Forget trying to break in. Forget my clearly lame backup plan of canvassing the entire town—school, streets, hospital—and freezing my feet off in the process. Instead, all I have to do is make friends with some girl.

But she's no longer shaking in the doorway, and I'm half out of my seat trying to figure out where she's gone when I notice that she's plunked down at the other end of this very table. Ha ha. Fate.

I raise my hand, start to wave it in her direction, and feel a shadow drifting over me.

Great. It's Logan. Just looking at her makes my head throb and a clump of tuna on whole wheat churn in my stomach.

Something flutters off her tray, a napkin, and she huffs out an annoyed sigh. It floats down, landing near my dusty feet, and I dunk my head under the table, take my time reaching for it. *How long can I hide down here?* I wonder. *How long will she keep waiting?* Finally, I suck in a breath, heave myself up, return the crumpled napkin.

"Thanks, Marsh," she says, but how she says it sounds more like *up yours.*

She's ticked off at me. Which God knows I probably deserve. I watch her flounce away, and then I remember New Girl. We lock eyes for just a second before her face gets pinker and she looks down at her soggy french fries.

Am I up for this? Making small talk with a girl? I gather my lunch stuff with one arm and slide it across the table before I can change my mind.

"Hey." I clear my throat. "We meet again."

She smiles. "Bus stop, right?" She says it in a soft drawl, so that *right* comes out in two syllables. "I'm Maddie Rogers, and I heard you're . . . um . . . Marsh Windsor?"

Can't think of anything to say for a minute so I stare at my apple. Clearly, I'm rusty at this kind of thing. I clear my throat again. "So, uh, what do you think of your house?"

"My house?" She lets out a light laugh. "Well, it's cold. It's old. The whole place looks like it's sinking into the ground. And it smells musty."

Her voice is so twangy when she talks, that without thinking about it, I start laughing.

Her cheeks get redder, if that's possible, and I can see now that it's not makeup. So I was wrong about that. It *is* natural freshness. Whatever that means.

Get back to the real issue, I tell myself, *that her house—the room downstairs—contains a doorway to another world.*

Not exactly sure how to bring this topic up, though—without scaring the crap out of her, at least. I open my mouth, but the stupid warning bell rings. Whatever her name is—I forget—New Girl is out of her chair in a flash. So I may have already scared her off. Or else I hurt her feelings by laughing in her face. I *am* rusty at this. But whatever, I'll catch her on the bus home.

I shovel my stuff into the trash, make my way around the tables, scraping my feet along, ignoring the stares. I have to walk by the sports tables to get out of here. Which means passing the football table and my former friends. That tuna sandwich is a damn brick in my gut because I know what they think about me. God knows I probably deserve this too. I turn my head to make it easier for all parties concerned, but when I do, I end up facing the lacrosse guys.

They're splayed out, not taking the bell seriously, huddled up in some intense conversation. One guy, a guy I don't recognize, squints at me, and the guy next to him, a guy I do know, unfortunately, Brad Silverman, smacks the stranger on the back.

"Yeah, that's him," Brad says. He lets out a snort and looks away, but the stranger doesn't.

He's a pretty big guy, I can see just in that second or two that we stare at each other. And he's blond with a square jaw and a blank expression. So he'll fit right in with Brad and his Neanderthal buddies. Only difference is he's got pink cheeks. I don't know why it takes me another second to figure it out: it's New Girl's brother.

Afternoon, I forget about her until it's our stop. I stand. Notice her across the aisle a few seats up, not moving. Her head's pressed against the grimy glass. Lindsay and Heather shoot by like they're on fire. One of them elbows me in the side, yells, "Sorry, Marsh." And they're both out the door.

But I'm blinking down at New Girl. What, is she planning to ride the bus all day? I hover over her for a second and suddenly she scrambles to her feet. It hits me that she didn't know it's our stop.

I hold my hand out. "After you," I say. It comes out like a bark, but the girl smiles and thanks me. A blast of cold air hits our faces when we step off the bus. New Girl cranes her neck around.

"Uh," I say. "We're that way."

Her cheeks blaze up.

Probably because I'm grinning like a maniac. *Is this it— this girl—my key into the thin space?* Who knows. But I stroll along with her toward Mrs. Hansel's house and keep grinning, even though the icy sidewalk's practically burning the skin off my feet.

4
I'm In

Say something! "I've been in your house."

New Girl's head snaps up.

"I live three houses down from you. Knew the lady who lived there. Used to help her out before she . . ." I stop, wondering if I should get into all this, but she nods.

"I know. She died. Last night, this neighborhood watch lady came over and told us all about it."

"Mrs. Golden," I mutter.

"Right," she draws out the word. "She was very, um, neighborly. She gave us a big basket with cleaning products and flowers and a pie." She says pie so it sounds like "pa."

I cough out a nervous laugh, and she shivers, clutching her thin jacket around her chin. I notice her glancing at my feet, which truth be told feel like frozen blocks strapped to my legs.

"I don't like shoes," I tell her. "They're restrictive."

She just nods. We're in front of Mrs. Hansel's house—
New Girl's house now. "You want to come in?" she says, and
I almost fall over on the sidewalk.

Can it be this easy?

"We're not half done unpacking," she says as she fiddles
with her keys. "You're going to laugh at how messy it is."

"I won't laugh," I promise, even though I can feel it already
burbling out of me. *This is it,* I'm thinking. *Don't blow this.*
I flex my feet, rub the soles across Mrs. Hansel's old welcome mat. They're numb, buzzing. Every muscle in my body
is twitching.

When the door opens, the smell hits me: Mrs. Hansel's
powdery scent mixed with medicine crossed with some kind
of piney cleaning solution. Then the cold. Or really the lack
of expected warmth. "Whoa," I say, making an exaggerated
brrr sound.

"I know," New Girl says. "My mother thinks the furnace
is broken. It's even colder upstairs."

I sway in the entryway, shoving my hands in my pockets
so she won't see them shaking. I'm three strides into the front
room, focusing on the fireplace, when my foot hits something. An open box. That's when I notice the room is full of
boxes and furniture. There's a couch wedged over the space
where Mrs. Hansel's bed used to be.

"It's slanty," New Girl says, reminding me she's still there.

"What?" I squint at this obstacle course, wonder how I'm
going to plow my way across the room.

"The floor. It's slanty." She tilts her head toward the chaos.
"We're probably just going to keep all the furniture against

the fireplace since it's going to slide down in that direction anyway."

"Huh?" My heart's slamming so loud in my chest, she's got to hear it. But what do I care? I hardly know this girl. I flex my feet and take another step, nudging a box aside with my knee. I'm about ten feet away from the fireplace. All that stands between it and me are two couches, a coffee table, and about twenty boxes. What's the right way to do this? Do I just climb over, move the boxes, step in—

"Is your house like this—slanty?"

"Uh, no." A laugh escapes.

"Hey, you want a snack or something?" She starts walking down the hall. I watch her ponytail swish back and forth. For a second I'm flashing back to Kate and Logan. How their ponytails did that too. I shake the image away because New Girl's chattering.

"Don't you just love this? Now here's a room that says fruit explosion."

I blink at her. She's waving at something in the kitchen. "Well?" she says. It sounds like *whale*.

I don't know what she's talking about. I drag myself toward her, poke my head into the room. I guess she means the wallpaper? Never really noticed it before, but she's right. The pattern's got every kind of fruit spattered across it—grapes, apples, oranges, and some unidentifiable greenish fruit that might be melon.

"It's a miracle there's still some left," she says, pulling a half-eaten pie out of the refrigerator. "Sam inhaled most of it last night."

"Sam?"

"My brother. You want a piece?"

I look over my shoulder, down the hallway. Which leads to the front room. Which leads to the thin space. Can I be this close? Again? And not take advantage of it?

"Pie?" she drawls.

"Pa," I hear myself repeat. "Yeah. Sure." What the hell is wrong with me?

We sit across from each other and eat pie—it's not half bad. Thanks, Mrs. Golden! And I tell myself I'm being productive by dragging my feet back and forth across the floor. I know the thin space is in the other room, but who's to say there isn't another gateway in this house?

"The lady who used to live here," New Girl says. "You knew her?"

Ha ha. You don't know the half of it. "Yeah. Mrs. Hansel was an interesting person."

"I'm sorry," she says, and I don't know why at first. The thing is I did like Mrs. Hansel once I got to know her. And the last time I saw her, after the accident, she was the only person who—

The front door slams and a deep voice calls out, "Hey." The guy striding down the hall has a lacrosse stick slung over his shoulder, all his gear dangling off it in a neat little pack. "Madison?" he says. He stops in the kitchen doorway when he sees me.

I rise partway out of my chair.

He thrusts out a hand. "Marsh Windsor, right?" He gives my fingers a twist before letting my hand go.

"You're, uh, Sam," I say. I was right. He's the guy I saw at lunch. Close up, his cheeks aren't pink like his sister's. They're red, which just makes him look mad.

He props his lacrosse stuff against the counter, grabs the pie tin off the table. "Heard you play football."

"Not this year," I say.

"Heard that too," he grunts out the words, openly gaping at my feet.

My toes twitch self-consciously. "You're going out for lacrosse?"

"Yeah. Played defense last year in Nashville."

"Nashville. Cool," I say, like I've been there. This small talk is killing me. Plus, I'm getting the feeling Sam's not too thrilled about me being in his kitchen. "Well, it was nice to meet you." I stand, nod at Sam, who's shoveling a chunk of pie in his mouth with his fingers, and then I force a smile in the general direction of his sister. "See you later"—I have to think for a second what her name is— "Madison."

She springs out of her chair. "Maddie," she says. Which gets Sam laughing for some reason and she flashes him a dirty look. "You can call me Maddie. Hey, let me walk you to the door."

Whatever. I follow her down the hall, but I have to stop in the entryway, take one futile step into the front room. A voice in my head says that if I have to wait, I can. I've waited two months already. She's invited me in. She'll invite me in again. Maybe next time the front room will be cleared out enough that I can walk through—

"Bye, Marsh," she says.

"Baa," I say, and I laugh, even though what I really want to do is cry. Or bash my head against a wall.

—–—

My parents aren't home yet. In the entryway, I grab a towel, press it around my toes. They burn against the fabric. My mother's taken to leaving a clean towel by the door. Mostly she's ignored the barefoot thing, my father too, but I know it's bugging them. I try to make it easier by keeping my feet clean. If they saw how red they get, how dirty, they might try to put a stop to it.

Technically, my house is a place where I can wear shoes, or at least socks. I can say with complete confidence that it contains no thin space. I have been over every surface. Twice. But oddly enough I'm getting used to being barefoot, and in a way I wasn't lying when I told New Girl—Madison— Maddie—whoever, that shoes feel restrictive.

Upstairs, I flop down on the bed in my brother's room where I've been sleeping since the accident. I kick my feet out, and I guess I nod off, because it's dark when I blink my eyes open.

"Marsh," my mother's calling. She says it a couple more times before I finally push myself off the bed and head down-stairs.

My parents are trying. Still it's painful to be with them. Dinner especially. Like, my mother tries to make everything normal. She sets the table—minus one setting—the same

30

way as always. We eat at the same time every night. She cooks up the same big meals.

What's changed, though, is so huge that even she can't pretend it doesn't exist. At some point she pulled his chair away and tucked it behind the china cabinet. Other stuff has disappeared from around the house too. Some pictures of the two of us. This ceramic bowl I made in art class back in fifth grade. She thinks he made it, though, so it's gone. I don't tell her *his* bowl is still displayed on the coffee table in the front room. Whatever. Stuff like this—things getting mixed up— it went with the territory for my brother and me. No point getting ticked off about it now.

"Have a nice day at school today?" my mother says. She sits across from my father. I sit across from no one.

"This chicken is good," my father says.

"I'm glad you like it. Do you like it, Marsh?"

"Marsh? Do you like it?"

I nod.

"Getting colder out there. Down to thirty tonight, I hear."

"Thirty?" My mother and father pass each other meaning-ful looks.

"Might snow."

"Snow?"

Out of habit, I swipe my feet back and forth along the wood floor.

"Would you like another piece of chicken?"

"Marsh?"

How long can this go on? Three months since the accident. Three months! It's crazy how long—

"Marshall, your mother is talking to you."

"Marsh?"

mm

From my brother's window I can see Mrs. Hansel's house across the line of backyards. Upstairs, two windows glow like eye sockets. It's Mrs. Hansel's bedroom. A shadow flits across one and I wonder if it's Maddie.

Funny girl, I think as I flop into bed. Of course this makes me remember Kate and Logan and I get a sick lurch in my stomach. Ahh. Fun times with my so-called girlfriend. I don't know how serious we were. Not very, I realize now. But I liked her. You don't just get over something like that. Seeing a girl, seeing *your* girl, kissing another guy. And when that guy happens to be your brother—

Ugh. I can't keep thinking about this. I twitch my toes under the covers, stare up at the ceiling. My brother tacked this poster up there a few years ago. A rocket ship blasting off. I stare at the puffs of smoke coming out of the rocket tail, the blobs of white and gray swirling.

Misty, like how Mrs. Hansel described the thin space.

I climb out of his bed and press my forehead against the window. The light's still on in that house. It gives me a twinge of something I haven't felt in months. Hope?

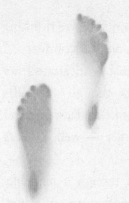

5
Mission

I time it leaving the house this morning because I want to catch New Girl on my way to the bus stop. I see a splinter of light at Mrs. Hansel's house, the front door opening, and a flick of a ponytail. "Uh." I clear my throat. "Maddie."

"Hey," she says. She wraps her arms around herself, hunches her shoulders. "It's freezing out here. This sure is different from Nashville."

Time to buy a warmer coat, I think, but what makes me an expert on keeping warm? I'm the idiot walking around barefoot. "Yeah," I say. "It's cold."

"Gray too." She blinks up at me. "Does the sun ever come out?"

Nope.

"Yeah," I tell her. "Usually. In the spring."

"I don't think I'll make it until then."

Me neither.

"I don't even own a winter coat. My mother bought me

this one before we moved. But I don't think she was thinking about the cold. That's my mother. Fashion over comfort ..." Her voice trails off and I watch the mist swirl around her face. "She was right about these boots, though." She lifts one foot and twitches it back and forth. "At least my feet are warm." Her face fires up. "I didn't mean—well, I wasn't talking—"

"Don't worry about it," I say, even though it feels like icy knives are stabbing my feet and shooting up my calves. We've reached the bus stop and we aren't alone. So that's that. Conversation with Maddie's over. Oh well. And here it was going along so great—weather, flaky parents, could it get any more fascinating?

"Marsh," Lindsay and Heather say together. They smile at Maddie. Apparently they've deigned to talk to her today.

"Your brother," Lindsay chirps up. "His name's Sam?"

"He's hot," adds Heather.

The bus rumbles up. Good thing too, since I'm not feeling my feet anymore.

Today I trudge through the front entrance of the school, pass the guidance office, notice Mrs. Golden's yellow head bobbing behind the window. She squints at me over her glasses and I pick up the pace.

I catch a glimpse of Maddie's ponytail turning down the sophomore hallway. Locker doors slam. The warning bell rings. I scrunched up my toes as I push through the crowd. Finally my feet are thawing, but now they burn and itch.

Maddie's stopped at a locker ahead, last one before the end. I give myself a pep talk. *Buck up. Talk to her. Get invited back into that freaking house.* But when I open my mouth, the "hi" dies in my throat. She's not alone. Her hulking brother's behind the locker door. He hisses something in her ear, and I head in the other direction, my blazing feet slapping the floor all the way to homeroom.

Lunch, I plunk down at that corner table again, unload my mother-made lunch—ham and Swiss on rye, an orange, an organic cookie—keeping one eye angled at the lunch line exit.

"Maddie," I say as soon as I see her. I notice her tray's not shaking today. Good. Time to get down to business.

"Hi," she says. It sounds like *ha.*

"Ha," I say back without thinking.

"Yeah, I know." She shrugs, sets her tray down across from me. "My accent. It's funny."

"I didn't mean—"

"No, it's okay. I've been hearing it all day. People want me to say stuff and then they make fun of me." She twirls a droopy fry in her fingers. "You have an accent too, you know."

"I—right, I guess it would sound like—so you're not used to the way—" I close my mouth. What the hell am I even trying to say? I puncture my orange with my thumb, gouge a line through the skin. Why did I think this was going to be easy again? I clear my throat. "I'm not making fun of you."

She looks down at her tray. "You're a junior," she says.

"Uh. Yeah."

"Like my brother." She twists her head, angles her chin in the direction of the sports tables. "Sometimes Sam's kind of

35

obnoxious. He gets like that around me . . . and my friends." She picks up another fry and taps it in a plop of ketchup. She's not looking at me, and I'm wondering where this conversation is going. "Do you have any brothers or sisters?" she says.

Okay, that's not where I thought this was going. The orange wedge in my mouth is a wet lump. I force myself to swallow it. "I had a brother. Twin brother, actually. He died. August. A few weeks before school started." I realize that I have not said these words to anyone before this moment.

Before I can stop myself, I'm flashing back. My white knuckles on the wheel. His skull thunking against the windshield. The glass shattering. How one side of his face blackened with blood and one eye—

"I'm sorry," Maddie is saying.

I must have closed my eyes. I blink them open. An orange slice is pulp in my fist. *Focus,* I tell myself. *Focus!* "Yeah, so I don't want to get into it."

"No. Right," she drawls.

I roll my organic cookie on the table. I can't eat it. It tastes like cardboard. *Say something!* "Sam, your brother. He's obnoxious you said?"

She rolls her eyes. "I'm his baby sister, you know? He doesn't like to see me as a girl."

"What's he like to see you as?"

She laughs, and I can't help cracking a smile.

"I mean he's weird about me being around boys, like I'm ten instead of fifteen. You know what I mean?"

"Yeah," I say, like I do.

"Anyway, I'm glad we moved. Stuff was cruddy back in Nashville." She twists her head again, frowns. "My mom's job got transferred, and she was like, 'Good.' She wanted a change. I don't know. Fresh start after the divorce."

"Sorry," I say.

"No big deal. It was a stepfather. She's been married three times. Long story."

"Okay." Her cheeks are killing me, how red they are. I yank a hand through my hair. It's getting long, keeps hanging over my ears, pressing on my neck. God, it's like how my brother used to keep his.

"—did some research online, looking for a nice suburb. And she found Andover close to the city and the schools are supposed to be so great."

"Yeah, great." I'm having a hard time following this conversation. Divorces? Suburbs? What are we talking about? And she's still going on.

"Sam was bummed about moving. But I was thinking, hey, maybe a fresh start for me too. Anyway, he's okay about it now and he's got a bunch of friends already. Like these guys from the lacrosse team were Facebooking him even before we moved, and he's got this carpool with them, and he said I could be in it too, but I want to do this for myself, you know. Make my own way."

"Right. Make your own way." I'm hardly listening anymore. I've been tapping my cookie against the table. There's only a chunk left. The rest is crumbs. "Your house," I say. I'm not sure this is the best tactic, but I don't care. "You settling in? Unpacking?"

She shrugs. "My room's mostly unpacked."

I remember last night, looking at the shadow in the window. "Which room is yours?"

"The one in the back corner with the two windows."

"That was Mrs. Hansel's room." So it was Maddie I saw last night. Not that it matters. Who the hell cares if I can see her room from my house?

"I don't really like it. It's freezing up there . . ." Her voice trails off.

"That sucks," I say, because it sounds like something a person who cared would say.

"You can see your breath. I'm not exaggerating. My mother called this heating maintenance guy, and he came over last night but—"

My eyes wander past her ponytail, across the cafeteria, to where her brother's laughing it up with Brad and his friends. *Maybe I should've taken that route,* I think. Tried to make friends with the obnoxious brother instead of—

"And last night I could hardly sleep, and then whenever I did fall asleep, I'd have these awful dreams and—"

I see that I'm going to have to get right to the point with this girl. "The front room," I say. "In your house. The one that slants—have you unpacked in there yet?"

"Oh," she says, startled. "We did get some stuff done last night. No thanks to Sam. He was just dumping stuff out of boxes and throwing it anywhere and I was trying to find a place for everything and I'm really not trying to be OCD about it, but you have to give some thought to arrangement— I mean feng shui, right?"

"Feng shui?" Why does she keep leading me off track?

"You know, like the placement of things in your house? Like how you're not supposed to have a bathroom in the center? Of course, upstairs we have that one pink-tiled bathroom in the middle, shooting out bad spirits everywhere."

I'm lost again and when the bell rings I heave out a sigh.

"Well, see you later?" she says.

A thought hits me. Something only halfway sneaky, but it might get me back into Mrs. Hansel's house and, with any luck, into the front room. "Hey"—I clear my throat—"maybe after school today, I could help you out with your unpacking."

6

I'm In, Part Two

I'm riding high the rest of the school day. My feet skim the halls, hardly feeling the dusty floors. *Forget this stupid school,* I'm thinking. No more searching around here for a thin space. No more searching anywhere. In a few hours, I'm out of here.

Flip open my locker, shove all my books in. No homework where I'm going. Ha ha. I slam the locker door and turn fast, thudding right into Logan of all people. She makes a little gasping sound.

"Marsh."

"Excuse me," I tell her, keeping my eyes fixed on my dirty toes.

"Wow. I didn't see you."

"Sorry." The word hangs there. I clamp a hand against my stomach then whirl away from her, turn the corner.

"Marsh!" I hear her high voice over my shoulder. What, is she stalking me now? "You can't keep blowing me off, you know. You—"

I turn the corner, elbow through a group of cackling girls.

"Just listen, Marsh. Please. I need to talk—"

I speed up even though a part of me wants to turn back, shake her, tell her it's time to get over it. Which is probably ironic coming from me. Plus, it's not really fair. How much of this crap is Logan's fault?

But forget her. Not my problem. I'm practically out of here. My whole body's vibrating when I climb on the bus. So close now I can't take it. My feet tap the grimy bus floor. *Almost there. Almost there.* The words pound in my head like a mantra.

Maddie sways in the aisle. She hesitates and then sits down next to me. "Sam's got some lacrosse meeting after school," she says, and I let her chatter drift over my head.

I'm thinking about logistics, how it's going to work when I get inside Mrs. Hansel's house.

"And my mother's working until—"

If the room's still full of boxes, I'll have to push stuff out of the way. Because I'm not going to fool around this time. No small talk or snacking on pie. This time I'm not blowing my chance. Step in. Get out. That's the plan. And whatever this new girl thinks about it, I don't care.

"Yeah, so there's a lot to do and it's really nice of you—"

I wonder what her face will look like when she sees me disappear. When I hit the thin space, and my feet press against the floor and—

"Marsh?"

Now I'm the one zoning out at our bus stop. Lindsay and Heather hover by our seat, waiting, it seems, for Maddie and me to stand up. Their heads bump against one another's and they whisper something that makes Maddie's cheeks burn. Who cares? Lindsay and Heather aren't bugging me today. Nothing is.

"Bye, Marsh," Lindsay calls over her shoulder. "Bye, Maddie."

"Bye, y'all," Maddie says.

A manic laugh heaves out of me. *Almost there. Almost there.* My feet thwack the sidewalk. Some part of me knows this is probably painful. A bigger part doesn't care.

Maddie is rummaging in her backpack while I rock back and forth on the front steps. She sighs, unzips one of the pockets, sighs again. "Shoot. Where's my key?"

I can't take this. *Come on.* I peer over her shoulder, try to get a peek of the front room from the window. But the glass is black and all I can see is my face. Eyes squinting. Jaw clenched. Take away the longish hair and, really, I look nothing like him.

"Oh, here it is." She flashes the key, jiggles it in the lock.

The familiar smell—medicine, powdery Mrs. Hansel—jolts me back to the last time I saw her. Her body shrunken and pale. Her hair just white wisps on her head. How different she looked. I gasped out loud, and there was Mrs. Golden, her sharp voice saying, *Look, Rosie, Marsh Windsor's come to visit you.*

And Mrs. Hansel, propped up in the bed by the fireplace, narrowed her eyes.

You remember him, right, Rosie? The boy from down the street who helped you around the house. The boy with the twin brother who—

43

Mrs. Hansel shook her head. It didn't seem like she remembered me.

Maddie drops her backpack on the floor. "Your, uh, feet are a little wet," she says. "You want a towel or something?"

I stare over her head toward the fireplace, and it's like the bed's still there. Mrs. Hansel's in the pillows like a shrunken up doll. That day, that last time I saw her, with Mrs. Golden hovering over her, telling me it was time to go home, that I was tiring Mrs. Hansel out—suddenly Mrs. Hansel didn't seem so tired. She lifted one pale hand. She said—

"They must be cold, your feet," Maddie is saying. "I'll go get a towel."

"Okay," I hear myself say. I am stepping into the room. The way across isn't blocked today. The pieces of furniture— the couches, coffee table, end tables—are arranged now and not just left wherever the moving men dropped them. Boxes line the walls, but I don't look at them. My eyes are on the floorboards, which run across the room toward the fireplace. *Like roads*, I think, *leading me to where I need to go.*

To end this. To fix this.

Somewhere, Maddie is laughing. "Now where did she put the towels?"

I feel the room slope down as I move. The space in front of the fireplace doesn't look special. The wooden floorboards are the same as all the other boards. Yellowish brown. Scuff-marked. My leg trembles when I lift it. I don't know what I expect to happen. Now that I am actually about to step in—

"I found a hand towel. That should work."

I press down. Watch my foot as it touches the wood. I imagine the floor will spring up to meet my sole, will give like a sponge.

Instead, nothing. The floor's as hard and cold as the area around it.

"Marsh?"

Holding my breath, I slide my foot to the side. And a slide in the other direction. Still holding my breath. Waiting.

"Marsh?"

I imagine my body being jerked from the room. My stomach tightens, anticipating the tug. *Here goes.* I have been planning this moment for two months. Since I stood over Mrs. Hansel's bed, my leg in a brace, my forehead itching with scars, the bruises on my nose barely healed.

I'll make a thin space, she whispered.

But where is it?

I suck in another breath. Shuffle back. Shuffle forward. Take two steps now.

Three.

Four.

Maybe I'm over too far? The bed was in front of the fireplace. I know that. So why am I still standing here? Mrs. Hansel said this was where she came through. And I know it's where she left the world. I saw her in the bed. Right here.

I whirl around, dragging my feet, drawing overlapping circles, moving out farther into the room. Maybe the bed wasn't directly in front of the fireplace. Maybe it was off more to the side? Is the space smaller than what I've been imagining?

I'm still here.

"You should sit down." Fingers brush my arm. "You look like you're going to pass out."

Why the hell am I still here?

Maddie's face hovers over me. Somehow I am on the couch, leaned back, blinking up at her. "Marsh?" she says. "Are you sick?"

I close my eyes. What if Mrs. Hansel was wrong? What if her soul didn't come through in front of the fireplace? How could she even know something like that?

Or worse. What if she was wrong about everything? What if she really *was* crazy? What if there are no thin spaces? What if I can't go—

"You're scaring me." The voice is soft.

I realize I'm shivering. My stomach tightens. Jeez, am I crying? Somehow there's a blanket over me. A warm hand flutters over my forehead.

"Walking around barefoot," she says, "you'll catch your death of cold."

What a joke. Death. If it were only that easy.

"What's so funny?"

I open my eyes. Maddie's face is very pale. Even her cheeks. "Nothing's funny," I tell her. And isn't that the truth? I claw the blanket away. Heave out a sigh. Even though I just told her nothing was funny, I laugh. The alternative is to sob. Rip this long hair out of my skull by the roots. Because here's what I'm thinking: *What if I'm stuck here?*

Forever?

"Is there anything I can do?" she says. "To help you?"

"I don't think so."

"What?" she says, because I'm laughing again.

"Not unless you know something about ancient Celtic beliefs."

"Celtic beliefs?" she repeats.

"Right. Didn't think so."

"Are you making fun of me?"

"Nope." I grip the edge of the couch. Oh God. Now what? What do I do here? Am I back to shuffling around barefoot? Back to hoping I'll stumble into some random—

"Mom," Maddie says. She springs up from the couch. A tall woman strides into the room, her high heels clicking across the floor.

"Oh," the woman says in a singsong voice. "I didn't see you had company."

Maddie's face fires up. "Why're you home so early? It's only four o'clock."

"I have to meet the maintenance man. I told you that. He should be here any minute." She starts to shake off her long coat, and then changes her mind. "This is ridiculous. It's freezing in here. Sweetie, aren't you going to introduce me to your new friend?"

"This is Marsh," Maddie says.

"Well, how nice to meet you. Madison, is that my good hand towel?"

"Oh," Maddie says. "I was—" Her eyes flicker at me. "The floor was wet by the door and I—"

"That's not the towel for that," her mother says.

"But I couldn't find—"

47

"Well, never mind. I hope you remembered your manners." She flips her head so her blond hair swings over one shoulder. It's the same color as Maddie's. "Have you offered your friend something to drink?"

I clear my throat. "Uh, thanks, no. I need to be going. Nice to meet you too." I stand, stare at the floor in front of the fireplace. My stomach's still churning just thinking about it.

I did what I was supposed to do. I slid over the whole area. Why didn't it work? I can't let myself think what the implications are of—

"Are you sure, sweetie? Because it's no trouble. Madison, why don't you go on and—"

"Mom." Maddie tugs my sleeve. "Marsh said he had to go."

I'm surprised when she follows me out, closing the door behind us. "Sorry," she says.

I don't know what she's talking about.

She rolls her eyes. "My mother." She's got my sleeve clutched in her fingers. "Um, Marsh, I saw you in the room. When I was coming back in with the towel. You were . . . looking for something."

I raise my hand, ready to wave it at her, ready to wave her away, but I stop. My hand's frozen in midair, and beyond that is Maddie's face and the white sky. Snowflakes drift down, dotting her cheeks and her hair.

"What?" she says, her forehead wrinkling up.

Flakes land on the top of my feet. Each one melts, burns. I don't know if I can do this anymore. I feel something rising up out of my throat. A laugh again, I hope, because what will happen if I let myself cry?

My brother died in August.

Mrs. Hansel died in September.

Now, we are slouching through November.

A shudder rolls up through my legs, my stomach, my arms. I fist my hands, try to keep myself from losing it right here on the sidewalk. In front of Mrs. Hansel's house. Where, pathetically, I have broken down before. How long can I—

"Marsh."

That snaps me out of it. I feel the snow on my skin again. I see Maddie's face. It's heart-shaped. Like Kate's. Not like Logan's. My stomach twists up.

I start to turn, but she's still holding my sleeve. "I've got to go." I shake her off, move fast, slap my feet down on the cold sidewalk. I live only three houses away, but when I get home, I feel nothing from my ankles down.

—mm—

In the morning, my mother's ranting. I hear her in the kitchen. "He's not going outside like that. He'll get frostbite."

And my father's low voice. "What do you want me to do? You want me to hold him down? You want me to force him to put on shoes?"

I don't wait to hear the answer. I head outside. Not much snow on the ground, maybe an inch or so, but as soon as my feet hit the sidewalk, the cold slices my skin. I flinch, watch my breath puff out, pull my coat up around my chin. I keep right on walking past Mrs. Hansel's house, my feet thudding against the concrete. Each step shoots pain up my legs. The bus'll come soon. I can make it.

What choice do I have? All last night I went over it again and again. Right before she died Mrs. Hansel practically gave me a blueprint. Take off your shoes. Step in. I mean, how complicated is that? She did everything but rope the spot off for me. It was supposed to be where her damn bed was.

Assuming she knew what she was talking about, my options are the same as before. Get back into that house or run across some other thin space.

If Mrs. Hansel was wrong...

But I'm not thinking about option three.

No. It has to be an issue of technique. That's what I've got to focus on. Maybe I didn't cover the entire space. I could've missed a board. I could've lifted a foot up at the wrong moment. I was in a hurry. That was the problem.

At the bus stop, I march in place. The snow melts where I'm standing. I don't know how, though; my feet can't be warm enough to melt anything.

Lindsay and Heather come bopping up, take one look at me and at my feet and then step away to whisper at each other. One word scrolls across their faces: *crazy.*

7
Welcoming Committee

When the bus screeches up to the school, there's Mrs. Golden, of all people, waiting at the curb, waving something. It's not a pie.

She boards and nods at the bus driver, swivels her head around until she finds me. "Marsh Windsor," she says. What she's got are socks and a pair of blue plastic clogs in her hands. "Put these on."

My feet and face burn as I clutch my backpack straps, stand, hobble toward her.

"Put them on," Mrs. Golden says again. "Now, Marsh, or no one is getting off this bus."

Behind me someone starts clapping. "Don't!" And my fellow bus riders pick up the chant: "Don't! Don't! Don't!"

It grows wild as I take the socks, bend down to tug them on. The material scratches my toes. I shove my feet into the clogs and wince as they bite into my feet. I thud down the bus steps, half tripping over a mucky snowdrift at the curb.

Someone yells out the bus windows. "*Now* he puts shoes on." And the former chanters laugh.

"Well, come on," Mrs. Golden says wearily.

I follow her into her office. She closes the door, yanks a chair out for me. "Sit down. Take those off."

I open my mouth and then notice she's got a dishpan of water on the floor.

"That's lukewarm water," she says. "Dunk your feet in it before you destroy your skin. Do you want to do that? Is that what you're trying to do? Frostbite is serious, Marsh. So is hypothermia."

I stifle a gasp. My feet smolder in the water like I've stepped in fire.

"Keep them in there." Mrs. Golden drapes a blanket around my shoulders. She moves behind her desk, sits, faces me. "Okay. Let's have it. What's going on?"

I try to scrunch my toes, but I can't make them move. Flames lick around my ankles, up my calves.

"You know, your mother called me this morning. Frantic. Crying. Do you hear what I'm saying?"

I shift my feet and more pain shoots up my legs until I swear I can feel it in my teeth.

"I'm not saying you should be over this. It's not something you *can* be over. It's something that's going to hurt less . . . with time. I understand that, Marsh." She clasps her hands together. "I've lost someone important to me too, so I know what you're going through. I truly do. Losing Austin—"

I wince when she says the name, and the movement brings with it another stab of pain in my feet.

"—was horrible. He was a good person and he didn't deserve to die when he did, and the guilt you feel . . ." She frowns. "You know it was an accident, right? Somewhere inside, you know that. But if you don't, I'm going to tell you: It was an accident. Okay? There, I said it. Now you say it."

I keep my feet still, watch the water shimmering over them.

"I'm waiting. You're not leaving this room until you say it: It was an accident."

Mrs. Golden's hair is very yellow. Maybe she's trying to look like her name. If that's her goal, she's failing. Her hair's the color of lemons. Most of the ladies in Andover color their hair. I don't know why that is. Except Mrs. Hansel. She let hers go white. Once she told me it used to be red. Which was hard to picture. *My natural color,* she said. *Irish girl like me.*

"Marsh."

I flinch. She's probably serious about holding me prisoner in her office. She's leaned back in her chair, her hands clasped behind her big yellow head like she's got all the time in the world. "I want to hear you say it." Her voice is very soft. "It was an accident."

She's trying to break me down. I almost laugh. Like guilt is my only problem here.

"Marsh."

I swear, I think my head will explode if she says that again. I clear my throat, and just that little movement twitches my feet. I suck a breath through my teeth. Focus somewhere over Mrs. Golden's lemony head. "It was an accident," I say.

She smiles, pleased with herself. She's made a breakthrough with the school head case. "You know we all care about you. We really do. Your parents, the school. That's why we've been indulging this barefoot . . . fixation of yours." She smiles again. "I want you to know something. That first day you came back to school, Mr. O'Donnell was saying it was a dress code issue, that the school could be liable if you hurt your feet. And he worried that you'd be a distraction to your classmates. But I explained what you were going through. And see how he's given you space? A few weeks ago, I heard him defending you to the superintendent. So we're thinking about you, Marsh. We're on your side." She stands up. There's a folded up towel on her desk and she walks it over to me. "Why don't you dry off now?"

I take the towel, pat the red skin, trying not to press too hard. I can't feel my toes. Everything else is on fire.

Mrs. Golden beams. "See, all better." She picks up the balled up socks and the plastic clogs. "Let's put these back on, okay? Let's try wearing shoes for a while. At least now, because of the weather."

I feel like a doofball in these blue clogs. My feet are still tingling, like ants are crawling around under the skin. I probably did get frostbitten, which I have to admit is not a good thing. If I freeze my feet off, there's no way I'll ever make it into a thin space.

But clomping around in shoes feels like admitting defeat.

At lunch, I park it at the same back-corner table. It takes me a minute to realize I forgot my lunch at home. I shove a hand in my back pocket. Maybe there's some money tucked away in my wallet. I dig past the license, the photos, a couple of old receipts. It's weird seeing this stuff. A little painful slap from the past.

Take the driver's license. Why the hell am I still carrying it around? I should get rid of it. Shove it in a drawer somewhere. I can't imagine ever driving again. And I can't stand looking at the picture.

Here's a weird thing about being an identical twin—something maybe other people don't realize—we didn't see ourselves that way. Identical, I mean. Like one time we stood next to each other in front of the bathroom mirror and I was thinking, *Do people really think we look the same?* Because I didn't think we did. Other people, though, they mixed us up all the time. I know that's what makes it so hard for them. We were MarshandAustin, the twins. And seeing me now forces them to remember him. Like I'm his ghost.

"Hi, Marsh." Maddie sits fast, slumping low in her seat. "Do you see Sam?"

I scuff my clogged feet back and forth across the floor. "Sam?"

"Yeah. Over there." She whispers so I have to lean closer to hear what she's saying. "That table where the lacrosse team sits. Is he looking at us?"

I glance over her shoulder. The lacrosse guys have their
sticks out like they're about to set up a game in the cafeteria. I catch a glimpse of Sam's square jaw. "He's not
looking."

She lets out a sigh. "Good. I don't want him to see me."
She nudges her tray toward me. "Want some fries?"

"No, thanks."

"Have some, really," she says. "I'm too upset to eat."

I know I'm supposed to ask her why. But I don't have the
energy. I do take a handful of fries though, and she smiles.

"This morning, you know how I wasn't on the bus?"

That's news to me, but I nod.

"Those lacrosse guys Sam carpools with, he wanted me to
ride with them today. He doesn't want me to—He doesn't
like that I'm—" She turns her head, squints over her shoulder. "See, he thinks you're—"

I'm only halfway paying attention, but I know where she's
going with this. Without really thinking about it, I find
myself wanting to help her out. "Hey, don't worry about it. I
know what people say about me."

"You do?"

I twirl my finger around my ear, the universal sign for
"I'm a lunatic."

Maddie exhales a weak laugh.

"Really. Don't worry about it." I flex my feet. The plastic
shoes dig into my skin. But I have to admit, it's kind of nice
having warm feet for a change.

"They were talking about you this morning." She slumps
down lower. "And your brother."

I flick my eyes toward the lacrosse table again. There's Brad Silverman sprawled out, looking cheerful, chucking a ball back and forth in his hands.

"Telling these stories . . ."

"Stories?" My heart speeds up. I can't figure out why. It's not like I care about these people or what they say about me. I lock eyes with Brad Silverman.

Maddie's chin is drooped so low it's practically on her lunch tray. "About how you and your brother looked so much alike."

"Well, we were identical." I try to say it with a laugh but it comes out weak and shaky. I watch Brad stand, walk toward the other end of his table.

"That must be kind of weird, having a twin. Were you the type that dressed alike?"

"Nah. We tried to be different." I snort. "Except during football season when he cut his hair." I notice Brad's pushing past the other sports tables, still lobbing the lacrosse ball. Sam's behind him, not looking very cheerful. I'm half out of my seat, my feet pressing into the clunky shoes, as both guys stride toward us.

"Madison," Sam says. "What the hell?"

The cafeteria is a rapt audience. Like someone turned off a switch. The usual roar fades out. Kids coming through the lunch line doorway freeze. At tables up and down the room, people snap their heads in our direction.

"Sam," Maddie says, bowing her head. "We're just eating."

He hooks a finger around her tray and tugs it toward him. His eyes are on mine. "I told you this morning, you can sit with us."

"Yeah, we want you to," Brad says, smirking.

Sam glares at him before turning back to Maddie. "Come on," he says, picking up the tray. "You're not sitting with this . . ."

"Freak," Brad supplies helpfully.

"I can sit with whoever I want," Maddie says in a quiet voice.

"We talked about this," Sam hisses.

People are out of their chairs now, pushing closer, like fans rushing the stage at a concert. Too bad we don't have microphones.

Brad's somehow elbowed his way over to my side of the table. "Nice shoes," he says.

I get a queasy flash of déjà vu, back to seventh grade when I once took a pop at Brad. That was the year he and my brother kept getting into it. Who knows why? Then somehow, I got dragged in. Another perk of being an identical twin. I'm minding my own business, cutting across the middle school baseball field and Brad comes hurtling out of nowhere, throws himself on my back. He'd mixed us up, is what happened. I defended myself. What the hell else could I do? Funny thing, Brad always thought it was my brother who gave him the split lip.

"What are you looking at?" Brad says. "Marsh," he spits out the word.

My brother had cracked up about that. *Hey. You're building up my reputation, little brother. The way you took him down. And I didn't even have to break a sweat.*

"That's right, I'm talking to you." Brad pokes a finger at my chest.

Just like last time, Brad's mouth plops open like a dumb fish. Just like last time, I'm surprised at the pain in my knuckles.

A girl screams. At first, I think it's Maddie, but there's someone else digging her fingers into my arm. Great. When the hell did Logan show up?

"Marsh," she wails. "Stop."

The audience is on their feet. Some of them applaud. Brad's sprawled out on his back, his fingers clutching his mouth. His lacrosse player buddies hover over him. Sam's dragging Maddie through the crowd. Her face is drained, white.

"Marsh," Logan says, "please, don't."

Don't what? I look at my fist, and somehow it's pulled back again.

"Hey, man, take it easy." Now my old pal Chuck's at my side, his mouth stretched into a grin. "Everyone wants to punch Brad, but maybe the cafeteria isn't the best place."

"It's not funny," Logan says. Her fingers are talons around my arm.

I yank away from her. I can't find Maddie. Too many people are pushed against the table. Mr. O'Donnell's bald head bobs through, and the crowd parts like the Red Sea.

For the second time today, I find myself sitting in Mrs. Golden's office.

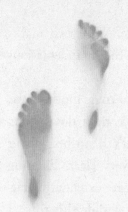

8
Wreck

She seems more upset than I am.

"I don't understand," she says, shaking her head. "We had such a nice talk this morning."

I'm plunked down in the same chair as before. I notice the dishpan turned over on another chair, the towel draped over it. I can feel Mrs. Golden staring at me and I force myself to turn my face in her direction. I notice her desk is overflowing with clutter. Besides a bunch of framed photos of her cuddled up with some smiling old guy, there's vases stuffed with flowers. A tin of cookies. Box of candy. Stack of greeting cards. Like she's the Welcome Wagon for the whole school.

"Marsh."

I've got my hands on my lap and I can't figure out why my right hand is throbbing. I look down at it—

"I know you're upset. But fighting? Really? It's not like you to—"

—notice the slice along my knuckle. Well, two marks really, now that I'm examining it. Nice. They're indentations from Brad's teeth.

"Of course, I called your parents. Your mother was extremely upset. She was ready to drive right down here. Your father too. And Mr. O'Donnell's disturbed about this new development. The rules are very clear. Fighting equals a four-day suspension. But there are extenuating circumstances, and so we're willing to let it slide this time. I understand that the other boy was provoking...Marsh. Are you listening to me?"

I try to look at her, but a freak ray of sunlight from the window glints off her glasses and I have to shut my eyes.

"Maybe we've been handling this the wrong way," she says. "Maybe we've let you go on too long. I know you were seeing a therapist after the accident. It might be time to look into that again. Or you and I could set up regular appointments during school hours." When I tilt my head back so she won't catch me rolling my eyes, she clicks her tongue. "There's no shame in talking to someone about what you're going through."

I stare at the ceiling. There's a gray blotch up in the corner. Probably some kind of fungus.

"We might be able to help you work through this."

"Yeah," I say, like I'm considering it. Like I didn't spend weeks slouched across a couch while some guy droned on about how I should open up, express myself, let it all out. Ha ha. Like talking about this crap is going to fix anything. But at least it got my parents to back off. Not that it mattered.

Since by that time I was working on my own solution to the problem.

"We could start today." The sunlight's gone now, and behind her glasses, Mrs. Golden's eyes are like slits. She leans forward, smiles. "You want to tell me what's going on?"

Nope.

But I can see the best way out of here is to throw her a bone. "It's sort of embarrassing," I say, "but this girl . . ."

Her face lights up. "A girl? This is about a girl?" I can guess what she's thinking: Girl problems, now that's an area she can deal with. Crazy guy walking around with bare feet, well, that's another story.

I half listen as she lectures me. Teen relationships. Competition. Jealousy, blah blah blah. I keep fingering Brad's teeth indentations on my knuckles. I'm not clear about why he was messing with me today. Well, okay, because he's an ass. But that's common knowledge. The real question is why I lost it like that. When Mrs. Golden finally sets me free, it's still bugging me.

―――

Missed the bus, but I don't care. My clunky plastic shoes skim the slushy sidewalks. These aren't the best footwear for snow. But they're keeping my feet somewhat warm and dry. Anyway, I'm not sure if a thin space is accessible if it's covered with snow. One more thing I don't know the answer to.

When I reach the corner, instead of heading toward my house, I clomp off in the other direction. I've got a vague idea where I'm going, but I try to put it out of my mind. Brad's expression when I clipped his mouth keeps flashing in my head. I don't know why he was surprised. He was in my face. He poked me. He had to expect that I'd react to that.

Or maybe not. I haven't been reacting to much lately. The twisted thing is that it felt good. That minute of rage, my fist against his face.

But this isn't me. *It's not me.*

My head knots up and I push my throbbing fist against it. The sky is white, just one big cloud, like a bowl flipped over the world. No sign at all of the sun when I cross the street. It's not a busy intersection. That night it seemed dead too. I thought we were the only car sliding through.

I wasn't paying attention. Only one part of me was gripping the wheel, watching the road. When the other car turned, the headlights whirled in an arc, blinding me. When I could see again, I was kicking the brake. But all the while, I was watching his face too. How bright it was in that light, how his mouth stretched open, how his eyes widened. He grabbed my arm. No sound for a second, and then the crunch of metal, and his body pushing forward, his face still turned. He was staring at me when his head struck the glass.

Drunk driver, I found out later. It was almost stereotypical how it played out. Guy on his third DUI, hurtling home from a bar, ran a stop sign. Turned left going fifty miles an hour. Of course, that guy stumbled away from the wreck. Don't they always?

Too bad my brother wasn't wearing his seatbelt.

See, Mrs. Golden, that part was my fault too. Get it? He unbuckled his seatbelt because of me.

I stop, suck in my breath, try to push my mind past it, but a little seeps through. *Look. When are you going to get over it? That's the way it is. It's how it's always been. You know what? Just freaking stop the car and let me—*

Out.

Somehow I'm leaning against a light pole at the intersection. The metal jabs into my back. My feet are sunken into slush. My socks are wet now, my feet icy. It was stupid to come here. If there were a thin space, it would probably be *inside* the car. Technically, that's where he left the world.

According to the rules though, it wouldn't be enough. He would've had to come through there too. We didn't even own that stupid car until last spring. Big sixteenth-birthday present from our parents.

I am sick of these rules. It's too hard to make a thin space. Too hard to find one. In the end, all roads lead back to Mrs. Hansel's house, and there's nothing to do—nothing—but get back in there and try—

"Marsh?"

I jerk my head around. Is that Kate?

She's slumped against a big oak tree at the edge of someone's front yard. I feel sorry for whoever lives there because after the accident, their lawn became the unofficial memorial site for my brother. Even now I see a few reminders sticking out of the snow. A frozen chunk of brown flowers. A half-deflated football. My mother comes down here, collects the stuff every few days. She doesn't want it to get rained on, she says. And now she's got it stacked up in my bedroom.

I used to come down here a lot at first too. But it wasn't to look at the memorial junk. Still had my leg brace on then, but I managed to drag my bare feet over the whole area. The stones on the street. The curb. It was a long shot. I knew that even then.

"I've never seen you here before," Kate says. She doesn't look at me, I notice.

"I've never seen you here either." I try to help her out by keeping my face turned to the side.

"I come here a lot."

Jeez, Kate. Give it a damn rest.

"It's really . . . hard for me." She keeps her eyes lowered like she's analyzing her boots. "I know it's . . . it must be hard . . . for you too."

You don't know the half of it.

"So if, well, I just wanted you to know that I wasn't trying to avoid . . . well, I'm just having a hard time . . . seeing—"

"I know," I say. Funny thing about Kate—once upon a time she was a cool girlfriend. Logan too. We were pretty lucky to have hooked up with them, really—twin brothers getting to date best friends. Or maybe Kate and Logan aren't friends anymore. I don't know about now, after everything. I get a sick image of us, outside the movie theater, and I have to shove my hands in my pockets to keep from pounding the light pole. Stupid, that Logan once called us a love square. Her chirpy phrase for the four of us, instead of a love triangle. Which she and Kate both thought was so clever and hilarious. Like, we were all friends and brothers and boyfriend/girlfriend and had so much in common. Even though we really didn't.

My brother and me, maybe we looked alike, but we weren't alike in other ways. He was the risk-taker, breaking the lock on the basement door. While I was content to sit out in the cold. He was more laid-back about stuff, except when it came to his room, which he kept anally neat. And I was the anxious slob. He . . .

But whatever. I could go on about all the differences. In the end it doesn't matter. People saw us how they wanted. To them, we were alike in the ways that count. Looks. Athletics. Academics.

Kate and Logan, maybe it's like that for them too. Both pretty, perky, popular. But I know Kate. Or I used to. She has this insecure streak that other people don't see. Had to ask a million times before we went out if she looked okay. Constantly fiddling with her hair, sneaking looks at herself in the mirror. One word and you could crush her. It made me like her more though, that vulnerable part.

Over by the tree, she's still studying her boots. The plush fabric is stained with snow. I could slide over to her now, put my hands on her shoulders, lift her chin—

My heart stutters just thinking about it. How many times did I look down at her, lean toward her, kiss her? I know the freckles spattered across her nose. I know her blue eyes, the shape of her face when it's tilted back.

And I know what those eyes look like closed. When she was kissing him.

She snaps her head up, like she can hear what I'm thinking. "I'm sorry." Her voice breaks.

The white sky blurs. I shut my eyes, feel snow wetting my face.

"I need to go." She pulls away from the tree. Has she always been so thin? The coat she's wearing swallows her up. She stumbles toward me, slipping a little on the slushy lawn. She stops a few feet away from me, pulls her hair back behind her ears, wraps a strand of it around her finger, a habit of hers when she's nervous. "I guess I'm not ready to ... Marsh ... I'm sorry ... I can't talk ..."

Her voice is a punch in the stomach. It reminds me why I can't give up.

Maddie's sitting on the stoop. When I reach the edge of Mrs. Hansel's driveway, she jumps up. "Hey," she calls. She wraps her arms around her flimsy jacket, crosses the lawn. "You weren't on the bus." She looks quickly at my plastic shoes. "Are you okay? Did you get in trouble?"

"Trouble?" I look past her at the house.

"After the fight," she says. "I saw the principal and then Sam wanted me to leave—I can understand what he's thinking, but anyway, I'm sorry."

Second time in thirty minutes I've got a girl telling me she's sorry. Must be my lucky day. "So, what's he thinking?" I blurt it out without planning to. I don't really care about the answer one way or another.

"He gets a little overdramatic sometimes, that . . . someone will take advantage, that I can't handle myself."

"Hey," I say, taking a step closer to the house, because I know what I've got to do. "We're getting wet out here."

"Can I ask you something?" She lowers her voice. "Logan . . . um, so I heard—I mean, is she your girlfriend?"

I sigh. "Logan?" I don't even know how to answer this question. It hits me that it's girls who have gotten me into this mess, who've started this whole crazy ball rolling.

"Are y'all serious? Because someone told me—Brad— he said that you've been kind of mean to her since the . . . um . . . accident."

"Brad?" I close my eyes and think about his mouth dropping open, his head falling back. I flex my hand, halfway enjoying the dull throb in my knuckles.

"He's in Sam's carpool. That was one of the things he went on about this morning."

The snow's really coming down now. The flakes plop on the ground fat and wet. "You think we should get out of this?" I say. "You know, go inside?"

She takes a step back and her foot slides in the snow. I reach out and touch her arm to steady her. "I don't know. Sam . . ."

"He doesn't want me in your house." Why does this surprise me? Has anything about this whole ordeal ever been easy? "So where is he?"

"Out with his friends, I guess. I don't know. I told him—" Maddie blinks at me. Snow wets her cheeks, her hair. "Hey, do you ever wish you could go back in time, do something over?"

I sigh again. Don't I wish that every second of my life? But I don't say that, of course, and I also don't say that if things go like I plan, right this moment, I'm going to get my chance. "Come on. You're freezing. Let's go inside."

We stamp our feet in the entryway. It's not much warmer inside the house, but at least it's dry. Maddie pulls off her jacket. "I'm going to grab another sweater," she tells me. She runs upstairs.

My heart's thumping when I kick off my clogs, peel off my socks. But now that I'm in here again, peering into the front room, my head's clear. This time it's going to work. This time it has to.

I march in, start at the corner, pace the floor. I walk the first wooden board, slowly, careful to press my foot all the way down, keep it there as I slide forward. When I reach the wall, I turn, leaving no gaps, and walk the next board.

Maddie's back in the entryway, but I pretend I don't see her. I'm on the fifth board, moving along like I'm skiing. When I hit the corner of a throw rug, I pause, nudge it up with my feet, and skim under that too. I'm not sure how rugs work with thin spaces. I'm not taking any chances.

Eighth board and Maddie's in front of me, blocking my way. She's wrapped in a sweater but still shivering. "Tell me what you're doing," she says.

I consider lifting her up, moving her out of my path. It doesn't seem right somehow. I don't know what *is* right anymore. "Please," I say, and I don't care that my voice cracks. "I have to do this."

She puts her hands on her hips. Then miraculously she steps aside. I'm past the section where Mrs. Hansel's bed was, way past it, but I keep going. Maddie helps me roll up the rug. When I hit the couch, she helps me push that out of the way too. I can't imagine what she's thinking.

I glide across the whole room. I don't stop until I'm in the entryway. Then I don't know what to do next. I sag against the wall. There's nothing to do but stuff my feet back into my socks and freaking blue clogs.

Maddie sways in front of me. "Marsh," she says.

I push my aching fist against my eyes.

"You're going to tell me now, right?" She draws the word out.

I am out of options. I let my hand fall to my side. I look down at Maddie. I don't believe I'm doing it. But I tell her.

9
Truth–Or Something Like It

We sit in front of the fireplace, legs crossed, facing each other. Maddie keeps chewing her bottom lip. "I'm trying to understand how it all works," she says.

Oh God. What possessed me to spill this story to some girl I hardly know? To some girl who without a doubt is thinking I'm the biggest lunatic she's ever laid eyes on? Who's got an overprotective brother who'll probably come after me with his lacrosse stick if he catches me in here with his sister?

I look down at the floor between us. I want it to swallow me up. I want to drop into it. Disappear. I am such an idiot.

"But I guess it makes sense, sort of, too," she says, and I blink at her. "A place where the same soul came in and went out. There's a logic to it. I don't get how Mrs. Hansel would know that, though. How she knew *where* exactly . . ."

"I know. My brother, he said the same thing to her. But she was sure of it. She had it all worked out." I can't believe I am having this conversation. Later I'll probably regret it, but right now, it almost feels good, throwing this stuff out there—stuff that's been knocking around in my head so long.

"Well, what did she say?"

Is she mocking me? She draws her knees up to her face, wraps her arms around her legs, waiting patiently, it seems, for my answer. I clear my throat. "Mrs. Hansel was born in this house. She showed us an old picture, her mother, pregnant, standing in front of the fireplace. She said something about that picture, her mother's smile—it just hit her that it was the moment she'd come through. And I know she died in the same spot. I mean, she made sure of it. She had the hospice people set up her bed right here." I trace my finger along the floorboards between us. "She knew she was dying and she wanted to die—to leave her body—in the same place."

"Ancient Celtic beliefs," Maddie says, her mouth twitching into a smile.

I feel my face burn. "That's what she said. You can look it up, you know, online. Thin space."

"I might do that," she says. "So, what are you going to do now?"

"Now?"

She shrugs. "You walked over every inch of this room and nothing . . . you know, happened. What are you going to do?"

I let out my breath, force a laugh. "That's the million dollar question."

"Why do you think it didn't work?"

I knock my fist against the floor. My knuckles are swollen up, purpling, but I hardly feel them. I'm remembering that the

head of Mrs. Hansel's bed was right here, the pillows probably just a little higher than where my face is now. When she
squinted her eyes, that last time I saw her, I didn't think she
recognized me. Because she was dying. Because I was pretty
messed up myself with my scarred forehead and dented nose.

But she leaned forward. She held out her hand. Jeez. She
sounded so sure of herself.

"I don't know," I say, and my voice is too loud for this
room. "But one time she told us a story about how she found
a thin space. She went into it."

Maddie's eyes widen. "Really?"

I nod.

"Tell me."

It's strange to hear myself say it. When I talk, I can hear
Mrs. Hansel's voice, quiet and twittery, in my head.

"She was only five years old when her father died. It was
unexpected, she said. One night at dinner, he complained
of a pain in his stomach. The next day, he was dead. Mrs.
Hansel's mother fell apart. There were days she wouldn't get
out of bed. She stopped taking care of Mrs. Hansel and her
brothers and sisters. Finally, their grandmother had to move
in to help out."

"Huh," Maddie says. Then she looks at me like, *go on.*

"Yeah, so the grandmother used to tell the kids these
creepy stories about growing up in Ireland. Stereotypical
stuff about leprechauns and pots of gold, but other stories
too, ancient ones about spirits in trees and haunted caves.
And she talked about thin spaces, where the wall between
this world and the afterworld is thinner. Mrs. Hansel got it

into her head that if she could find a thin space, she could go through and look for—"

"Her father," Maddie says.

I'm surprised to see she's following the story with some kind of interest. That or she thinks I'm nuts and she's humoring me so I'll hurry up and finish.

"You said she found a thin space," Maddie prods me. "Where?"

"Okay, so the grandmother told Mrs. Hansel about a house. It was in another town, down the road from the grandmother's, and a man had died in the upstairs bedroom. Anyway, after a while, Mrs. Hansel's mother got better, started taking care of herself and her kids again. The grandmother moved back home, and one day when the family went out to visit her, Mrs. Hansel snuck away to go looking for the place. She found it all old boarded up, but the door wasn't locked, so she let herself in and went upstairs. In the bedroom, she took off her shoes—because that's what the grandmother told her you were supposed to do—and she put her bare foot down on that spot. Immediately, the room disappeared."

"Disappeared?" Maddie raises her head. "What do you mean?"

"I don't know. She just said all of a sudden the room was gone, and she wasn't there anymore, in that house. She was somewhere else. It was misty, she said, and cold."

Maddie smiles. "Well, this house sure has that going for it. I'm surprised you haven't found anything here. I mean I can see my breath upstairs. I've been sleeping with like four blankets wrapped around me."

76

I knock the floor again and this time my knuckles blaze up in pain.

"Then what happened?" Maddie says. "Did Mrs. Hansel find her father?"

I nod. "He was wandering around in the mist, still wearing the same clothes he was wearing the night he said his stomach hurt. He hugged her. He told her everything would be okay."

"Huh," Maddie says.

Maybe I haven't told this right. It seems sillier than how Mrs. Hansel explained it. Now I'm imagining a little girl version of Mrs. Hansel skipping around in a fluffy cloud, talking to this nice dead guy, and it's hitting me that it could all just be a story—a story to make people feel better about death.

I cradle my bruised hand against my chest. There's a freaking lump in my throat. Reality is hitting me again. I can't deny it anymore. There's no thin space in this room.

Maddie's staring at me. She's thinking I'm crazy. And I must be. Crazy to have believed this stuff. Crazy to have told her.

"Marsh?"

I groan.

"You probably thought of this already, but that house Mrs. Hansel was talking about, the one she sneaked into when she was a little girl, have you ever tried to find it?"

I swallow, take a breath so I don't start moaning. "It's gone," I say. "Mrs. Hansel went back about ten years ago, after her husband died. He died in this house too." I notice her face brighten up, and I shake my head. "He's not from here. He was born in Canada. To make a thin space, the same person has to come through and go out in the same spot."

"That makes it kind of rare then, doesn't it?" she says. "I mean, how often can that happen?"

I laugh. "Not too often, apparently. That's the problem."

"But you said that she went back there, to the house."

"It was burned down, she said. Just the cellar was left."

"Did she walk around the place anyway?" She's talking fast now, waving her hands. "Maybe step around the general area where the bedroom used to be?"

Funny. My brother once asked the same thing. "It wouldn't work," I say. "Mrs. Hansel said the thin space was up in the air. The bedroom was upstairs. That's where the man's soul left his body."

Maddie's forehead wrinkles up. "I guess you couldn't find a ladder, you know, try to get in that way?"

I grunt out another laugh. "You sound like my brother. He asked her that too. She said you need a solid surface. You need to step onto it. Barefoot. He didn't believe any of it, but he kept asking her to explain. I think he got a kick out of the whole story. Plus, it was kind of boring, the stuff she had us doing around here. Those stories she told us made the time go by faster." I study the floorboard near my feet. There's an old burn mark, probably from a fireplace ash. "Neither of us believed her. But now I just—" My voice breaks. "I want to see him."

"Yeah," she says quietly. "I get that."

I keep looking down but I can feel her eyes on me, hear her soft breathing. I don't understand how this happened, how I came to be sitting on this floor with this girl. It's like

I'm waking up from a dream. Ha ha. Who am I kidding here? This is a freaking nightmare.

"Oh, crud," Maddie says, springing up and looking out the window. "Someone's home. Sam!"

I unfold myself from the floor. "I'll go out the back."

"Hurry," she tells me.

I duck out through the dining room, trip through the kitchen. I grab the doorknob at the same time the front door opens. I hear Maddie saying something about the snow, and then I'm stumbling down the back steps.

I skate through the backyards, glad again for these blue clogs. The snow's several inches deep now and still flaking out of the white sky. I'm out of breath, soaked, when I clomp into my house.

"Marsh," my mother says in a broken voice, and I fight the urge to tear back out into the snow. She's hunched over the sink, sponging a glass. "I talked to Mrs. Golden today."

The day flickers back at me. Morning: soaking my feet in the dishpan. Afternoon: punching Brad in the mouth.

I fall into a kitchen chair and tug off my coat. Unlike Maddie's house, our house is a steam bath. Or maybe I'm just overheated from my sprint through the backyards.

"Marsh."

I never know what I'm supposed to say.

"A fight? You got into a fight?"

My mother looks very tired. Or maybe she's always had purple smudges under her eyes and lines dragging down the corners of her mouth. Maybe I've never looked at my mother's face.

"Mrs. Golden said something about trying counseling again." She lowers her eyes, and now I notice the lines etching her forehead.

When you come right down to it, does anyone ever really look at another person's face?

"She thinks that maybe it's time for you—for the three of us—to talk to someone again." Her voice shakes. "It's been three months."

I study the knuckles on my right hand. Now the skin's swollen up around Brad's teeth marks.

"I miss him. I can't believe he's gone. I see you, and I see—" She's turned her back to me, sobbing, still dragging a sponge over the same glass.

I'm supposed to comfort her. You don't just sit there in front of someone—your mother—when she's breaking down. But I can't make my feet move in my plastic shoes.

"Austin," she says, and the word comes out like a wail.

In the hospital, she sounded like that too. When I opened my eyes and the light was so bright and my parents swayed over me.

I don't like to think of this. But like other memories, it sneaks through when it wants to. The cloying medicinal smell of the room. The nurse scratching something on a clipboard. The welcomed beep of pain medicine surging through my IV. The chair in the corner, a different person hunched over in it each time I opened my eyes. My father. My mother. One of the girls. Chuck or another guy from football.

No one had to tell me. No one had to say it. The wreck came back in pieces. Later. But only a few minutes after I woke up in that room, I knew my brother was dead.

"I know," my mother says. The glass shakes in her hand. "I know you don't want to talk about him."

I kick off the plastic clogs, peel off my wet socks. My sweatshirt too—I've got to get that off. It's damp with snow and sweat.

"I don't think it's right what we've been doing. Going on like nothing's happened. Pretending we're not thinking about him, missing him. I thought it was easier not to talk about it. But, Marsh—"

This room is so hot I can't stand it anymore. I yank off my T-shirt, ball it up in my fist.

"I think we have to. We have to get it out. Tell each other how we feel." She sets the glass down. She bows her head in front of the sink. "Just let it out."

I can't breathe in this heat. I may have to take off my jeans. A thought slides through my head: What if.

What if I *did* just let it out. If I told my mother what I've really been up to lately. And why.

But I know I can never do it. Just like I know I'd never strip down to my underwear in the sweltering kitchen. I stand up. "Mom," I say, and I'm happy to hear my voice comes out halfway normal. "I miss him too."

Hug her, I tell myself, *just hug her and get it over with.*

So I do that. My mother and I rock together, and when it seems the appropriate number of seconds have passed, I step away.

10
Boots

Morning, I make a show of my boots. They're my brother's really. I found them in the back of his closet. I clomp down the stairs, the laces trailing on the steps. My father notices them right away. He's in the hallway straightening his tie in the mirror.

"Good morning, Marshall." He looks like he wants to say something else, but he nods instead.

I nod back and do a quick tromp through the kitchen so my mother can feel better about our lives too. She smiles when she hands me my lunch bag.

"See?" she says, sneaking a glance at my feet. "It was good that we talked yesterday."

The wind burns my face when I open the front door. I brace myself for another gray November day. There's a nice layer of snow plastered over everything. I trudge down the front steps. Looks like my father's already shoveled. Once upon a time this would've been our chore. *Why do you think I had two boys?* he used to joke. *Free manual labor.*

Ha ha, Dad, my brother always said back.

—~~~~—

These boots are heavy, like I've got rocks strapped to my feet. My mind's numb today. I'm tired of thinking, feeling. My mother's teetering on the edge of a breakdown. My father's probably just flirted with a heart attack by shoveling. There's no thin space in Mrs. Hansel's house. I punched someone in the mouth yesterday. What else? Am I forgetting anything?

When I reach Mrs. Hansel's house, I remember. Maddie. The thought makes my stomach cramp up. By now, she's had enough time for the things we talked about yesterday to sink in. I picture her shivering upstairs in her bedroom questioning my sanity.

Her front door slams and someone whirls out, skids on the stoop, grabs the railing. Maddie's mother. "Yoo-hoo!" she calls. "Madison's friend!"

I twitch my head into some semblance of a nod.

"You don't happen to have an extra shovel by any chance?" Her accent's thicker than Maddie's, so *chance* comes out like *chay-unce.* "We don't own one. In Nashville we could make do without."

I clear my throat. "I'll go get it."

"Aren't you a peach," she says.

Before I'm halfway back, I see Sam crunching across the yards to meet me. "Thanks," he grunts. He grabs the shovel

84

then stomps over to his driveway to dig out his mother's car.

"The roads look bad," she says to Sam. "I can't believe they didn't call school."

"People here know how to drive in snow," Sam says. He's scraping the shovel back and forth, leaving a trail of snow clumps behind him.

"Well, it makes me nervous."

Sam mutters something under his breath.

Maddie slips outside then. "Oh," she says when she sees me.

"Madison, get over here," her mother says. "I'll let you clean off the back window for me."

I'm already past the driveway when I turn to see Maddie dragging her arm across the glass. I don't know what I'm thinking, but I stride back, step between her and the car, and swipe the snow off fast. I can see her out of the corner of my eye, shivering in her thin jacket, looking down at my boots.

She leans toward me, whispers, "Are you okay?"

Funny thing. I don't remember anyone asking me that in a long time. Another funny thing: I have no idea what the answer is. Before I can say anything, a horn beeps and a car rolls up to the curb.

"Ride's here," Sam says, thunking down the shovel. "Madison, let's go." Apparently, he's ignoring me.

Brad Silverman throws open the back door. His lips blubber out, fat and bluish. He's not ignoring me. We lock eyes and I can tell he's thinking about bailing out of the car and hurling himself at me. But Maddie's mother totters between us, waving the shovel.

"What a lifesaver you are, honey," she says to me. "I'll just leave this on the side of the house. You can pick it up on your way home." Then she turns toward the car. "Careful on these roads, y'all. My word, sweetie, what happened to your mouth?"

I don't stick around to hear Brad's response. I tromp off to the bus stop, still turning over my own answers.

Am I okay?

~~~

Now that I'm wearing something on my feet, I can't figure out what the purpose of school is. All semester I shuffled around imagining being sucked out of this place. Yeah, it was always a long shot, I know that, but there it was. Something to shoot for.

Today I clunk around like I've never seen these hallways before. Spilling my guts was stupid. Maddie was humoring me. She couldn't have believed me. *I* don't believe me. The proof was in the slanted front room of Mrs. Hansel's house. I can't kid myself anymore. I can't say that maybe I missed a spot or maybe the bed was pushed over or whatever. I'm still here. I slapped my feet over every freaking inch of that floor and I'm still here.

I move through the cafeteria, ignoring the buzz around me. I can sense the speculation in the air. Barefoot one day. Plastic clogs the next. Today, boots. What'll be tomorrow? Rollerblades?

I pass the football table, where a couple guys salute me. Next table over, the lacrosse players put on a little show for my benefit. They rise up together, a wall, their arms crossed in front of their chests. Brad cradles his lacrosse stick, puckers out his swollen lips as I clop by. I notice some of the guys at the football table rising too. Chuck flashes me a grin, gives me a thumbs up.

Has there always been this animosity between football and lacrosse? I can't remember. My brother and I played both sports in middle school. A lot of the guys did. In high school, though, it seemed like you had to pick one or the other. We joked about one of us going out for each team, so we wouldn't have to choose. Take turns. Switch places. In the end, we didn't bother, just stuck with football.

That kind of thing—switching—takes planning, energy. It's one thing to joke about it, another to do it. Plus there's the part about getting caught. We learned that the hard way in sixth grade when we tried going to each other's classes. *Man, we're in trouble,* says his voice in my head.

Trouble. Ha ha. He didn't know what trouble was.

Back-corner table, I plunk into a chair, drop my bag, dump my food out. Peanut butter sandwich. Banana. Some kind of cheese crackers. An organic candy bar. A folded napkin. I flip it open, half expecting to see a little note. My mother used to do that. Put silly messages in our lunch bags. Riddles. Funny sayings. Sometimes she'd write out our names in mustard on our sandwiches. She never mixed us up. That's one thing I can say about her, my father too. Our whole lives, they could always tell us apart.

"Marsh." Maddie sets her tray down across from me.

"Huh," I say. "You're . . . uh . . . eating lunch with me?"

She's sitting straight in her chair, not hiding today. "I talked to Sam this morning, to Brad and the other guys too. I told them I can I eat with who I want to." She bites her lip. "I mean if that's okay with you."

I glance over her shoulder, catch Sam's eye. His face is on fire. I turn back to Maddie and shrug. "Yeah, uh, sure."

I don't really know what else to say, so I start peeling my banana. It's got a black strip of rot running down one side. I pluck that part out and tear the rest of the peel off. I don't understand this girl. She's parked across from me like we're old friends, like I'm just a regular guy and not the madman skiing across her floorboards. I flex my feet, remember the clunky boots, and let out a sigh.

"I've been thinking," she says.

I bite into my banana.

"About thin spaces."

I cough, almost choking on a banana chunk.

She doesn't seem to notice. "You know how it's kind of hard to make a thin space because the same person has to come through and go out in the same spot?" She's talking faster now, waving her hands. "I started thinking about how you've been walking around barefoot hoping to find one."

I feel my mouth fall open. Luckily, I've already swallowed my food.

"But that would be almost impossible, right? I mean there could be a thin space anywhere. What are you going to do? Walk around every square inch of solid surface in the entire world? It just seems like you need a starting point, you know? So I did a little research."

I clear my throat. "Research?"

"Yeah, on thin spaces in general. There's really not much out there. But it gave me an idea. Did you know that a person died in the supermarket parking lot last week? That Goodfoods place off Main Street? A man had a stroke walking into the store."

I shake my head, not sure where she's going with this.

"So, I was thinking, why not start there? Instead of just stepping all over town with your bare feet randomly, or whatever you've been doing, why not check out some specific places where you know for sure that a person died? At least you've got half the equation right."

"Half the equation?"

She sighs. "You know for a fact a guy's soul left the world there. Maybe he came through there too."

"In front of the supermarket?"

"Why not?" She looks offended. "His mother could've gone shopping when she was pregnant. The store's been there for like fifty years. I looked that up too. The guy was only forty-three when he died, so it's possible."

"Possible." I shrug. What she's talking about, at least what I think she's talking about—finding these spots around town where people died—makes me feel a flicker of hope.

But I quickly tamp it down. I've been down that road before. Barefoot. I can't do it anymore.

She's still talking, fluttering her hands. "I found this obituary site online, for Andover and the county. And I realized that a lot of people die in the hospital. So maybe you could try there too. You don't know when or where those people came through, of course, but it's another possibility, right?"

"I already tried that."

"And?"

"And I didn't find anything. I took a bus out there last Saturday. I couldn't get into most of the rooms, but I walked around the hallways. It was stupid." As soon as the words leave my mouth, it hits me how true that is. Everything I've been doing has been stupid.

"What's the matter?" Maddie says.

"I don't know." I look down at my sandwich. I notice my mother's cut the crusts off the bread. The gesture makes me feel sorry for her and hate her at the same time.

"Are you okay?"

There's that question again. But now I know the answer.

It's no. It's always been no. Since I woke up in the bright hospital room. Since I drove through the intersection, my head pulsing with what happened with Kate and Logan. With what he did to me. And what I did to him. Since I wished for that one second that he—

"Marsh," Maddie says.

My knuckles throb against my sandwich, and I try to concentrate on that. I have a flash of myself lurching down a hospital hallway, holding the cheap flowers. How did I ever believe that would work?

"Are you going to try it?" Maddie says. "Go to the supermarket? Walk around the parking lot?"

The answer to this question is clear too. "No. I'm done with it. The hospital, walking around barefoot, in school, outside—all that was kind of my Plan B." This feels like a confession, and I can't help sighing.

"What was Plan A?" She's got her chin jutted out, and I figure she must know what I'm going to say.

"Look," I tell her, louder than I mean to, "I thought the thin space was in Mrs. Hansel's—in your house. Everything else was just a way to pass the time until I could get inside— get into your front room."

"Oh," she says. The color spreads across her cheeks. She shoves her lunch tray toward me and stands up. Like she's mad at me.

I don't know why. What does she care about my crazy plans?

"You wanted to get into my house," she says. Her voice is loud too.

Isn't that what we've been talking about? "Well, yeah," I say, and the ludicrous picture of myself kicking at the locked doors, staggering around in the dark basement, pacing the driveway plotting my break-in—all my scheming these past few months rolls out in front of my eyes. Could I have been a bigger idiot?

"Is that what this is about?" she says. "Is that what you—" But she doesn't finish the sentence. She snatches up her tray, whirls around, and dumps her uneaten lunch in the trash.

I watch her stride across the cafeteria, that perky blond ponytail swinging. When she reaches the lacrosse table, Sam's standing. He's probably been watching the whole time, witnessed what happened. Whatever that is. I have no idea. He grabs her arm, but she shakes him away and keeps on striding right out the door.

He turns back to glare at me. Talk about people dropping dead from coronary embolisms. The guy's head is about to blow off.

I rearrange my expression into something that I hope says, *Look, buddy, I didn't do anything to your precious sister.* Then I settle back into my seat. Any minute now, he'll probably come charging at me. Maybe Brad will join him and they'll both kick the crap out of me.

I deserve it. I roll through that scenario for a minute. The lacrosse players brandishing their sticks. The football players rising up to help. Other people throwing themselves into the fight. The ensuing chaos erupting in the cafeteria. And me, back in Mrs. Golden's office. Yet again.

I imagine her shaking her yellow head at me. *What are you doing, Marsh? Marsh? Marsh!*

And all I can hear myself answer is: *Nothing. I give up, okay? I give up.*

11
Something like Normal Life

The bell rings. I stand, looking quickly toward the lacrosse table, but no one seems like they're planning to jump me.

I'm getting that feeling again, that feeling that I'm waking up, that I'm figuring something out. It must be the boots. Wearing them makes me feel halfway like a person. I'm no longer looking for a thin space. That's what it is. My brilliant plan failed.

You're just a student, I remind myself, *just a regular person heading down the hallway. Going to your locker. Carrying your books. You're never going to be sucked out of this life. Accept it. Go to class. Talk to people.*

These are things I used to do. I could do them again. Participate in the world. Be Marsh Windsor. What the hell else am I going to do?

"Hey," someone says, tapping my shoulder.

Awesome. It's Logan. I consider ducking away, but my

boots hold me to the ground. This is reality. Another thing I'm going to have to face.

Logan's got a book pressed against her chest. An English book, I notice. We are standing in the doorway of the English class, after all. Logan is in my class, as she has been all semester—a fact that hasn't registered until this moment.

"I saw what happened at lunch," she says.

"Really?" I try joking with her. "Then maybe you can explain it to me."

She rolls her eyes. "So what's *with* her?"

"Her?" I know she means Maddie, but I'm stalling because of course I have no idea what the answer is.

"*Her*, Marsh, the girl you ate lunch with, the girl you've been eating lunch with for like, three days now. You want to explain that to me?"

"Explain?" I'm looking over Logan's head, at the people bunching up behind us in the doorway. "Come on," I say, touching her elbow. "We're causing a traffic jam."

"I don't care," she says. Her voice is very high and breathy. For some reason, I've forgotten this. "You keep avoiding me. I've been trying to understand. Trying to let you . . . I don't know, do whatever you have to do." She grabs her book, waves it. For a second I think she's going to whack me on the head with it. Instead, she points it at my boots. "I get we've had some issues, but last time I checked you were my boyfriend."

People press closer, some of them not bothering to hide their interest in our little conversation. Halfway down the hall the English teacher pushes through the crowd. "What's the hold up here?" she calls out.

Logan doesn't budge. She's blinking back tears. I've seen this look on her face before, and at this moment, I've got the same response: intense nausea.

I clutch my side. "Logan, I, uh, I mean, that girl and I—we—"

"Whatever about the girl. I want to talk about *you*—about *us*." She grabs my arm, jerks it. "After school. Okay? Will you talk to me after school?"

"Move it, people," the teacher says. Someone elbows me in the back. I'm getting shoved through the doorway.

Logan's fingernails dig into my forearm. "Okay?" she says. "Okay, Marsh?"

Her high voice makes my head throb. "Right. Later. I will." I tug away from her, almost trip over my bootlaces.

I go through the motions in class. Everything feels rusty to me—opening up my notebook, flipping the pages in my English book. I notice we're on page 156. Apparently, it's a story we were supposed to have read for today. I didn't read it. I didn't read any of the other pages before it. I rub my fingers over my notebook. The thing looks brand new. I haven't even written my name on the cover. I scrawl out *Marsh Windsor* now and grit my teeth as a wave of self-loathing crashes over me.

Logan's sitting across the room in the corner by the window. Maybe she sits there every day. I'm sitting by the door. Maybe I sit here every day too. I shrug away her stare. Hell yeah, I've been avoiding her. But what else am I going to do? Unload on her? Tell her there's nothing going on between Maddie and me? That I just wanted to get into the girl's house? That I thought there was a thin space? That I was freaking wrong?

Anyway, tomorrow I'll be eating alone. Maddie's mad at me, and she should be. She got a glimpse of what I really am. Now she can join the club, get in line. I'm the boy her brother warned her about. For all she knows I get into fights every other day. She can add that piece of information to everything else she's heard about me. The dead twin brother. The bare feet. It's clear I don't make the most stable lunch buddy.

The teacher drones on. She writes on the board. I copy the words down dutifully on my blank notebook page—something about truth with a capital *T.* I let out a sigh. That's my problem exactly. Truth.

Truth: My brother's dead.

Truth: I'm here. And there's nothing I can do about it because . . .

Truth: There is no thin space.

When the bell rings, Logan marches over to me. I take a breath and try to meet her eyes. I owe her that much at least.

At the end of the day, she finds me at my locker. I've agreed to let her drive me home. She waits while I rummage around for my stuff. I'm making an attempt to pack up the proper materials. Since I've woken up to reality, I realize that I'm behind in everything. I've waded through somehow. Gotten through my classes without failing, but I have no idea how I've managed that. This whole semester has been a fog. I, *we*—my brother and I—used to be good students. I guess that counts for something around here. Like I've stored up some goodwill along the way. The teachers have let me slide.

Maybe they've all done what Logan said—they've let me do what I've had to do. But that can't go on forever.

I shove some books into my backpack and then turn to Logan.

I'm trying to keep my eyes on her face, the way a normal person would. Jeez. I forgot how pretty she is. Her face is rounder than Kate's. Her hair is fluffier than Maddie's. It's blond too but with streaks of lighter color. Her eyes are green. She's got a beauty mark perched above the corner of her mouth.

She smiles at me. Her teeth are very white and perfectly straight. I remember she had braces for a while, all through middle school, now that I think about it. We walk outside, past the buses lined up, across the student parking lot. She stops in front of a sporty black car.

"Yeah," she says, and laughs. "My old car finally died about a month ago."

I climb in, wedging my backpack between my legs. The car's low to the ground, cramped inside. My knees bunch up in front of me.

"There's a button on the side," she tells me. "You can move the seat back."

I do that while she watches. The seat groans into another position. Now my legs are sprawled out, my head's tilted up, like I'm lounging in a lawn chair. I stare at the car ceiling. It's too hard for me to look at Logan. I remind myself of the point here. Reality. Truth. Or a version of it. All of which, unfortunately, includes dealing with her.

"So what do you think?" she says.

"Think?"

She flashes her white teeth. "Of the car. Do you like it?"

"Oh, yeah. It's great."

"I know. But sometimes, wow, I miss my other car. A lot of memories in that car." She edges her way into the stream of cars leaving the lot. Around us, horns honk. Brakes squeal. Tires crunch over the packed snow. "I know it's silly. The thing was a piece of junk. Do you," she says, her voice faltering, "ever think about . . . that car?"

"Yeah. Sure." I can't picture it, though. The only clunker I can see is the one my brother and I drove. In Andover a lot of kids get brand new cars—nice cars—when they turn sixteen. We were just happy to drive anything. The only annoying thing about it was sharing. But that's reality when you're a twin. You share.

"I'm sorry I lost it today," Logan says. "Outside English. I promised myself I wouldn't do that. I promised myself I'd wait until you were ready to talk to me."

I don't know if I can handle this. A confrontation with Logan in her new sports car.

"But yesterday, when you got in a fight with Brad, and then today when I saw you sitting with that girl—" She pulls a hand off the steering wheel, jabs it toward me so I have to press back into my seat to avoid injury. "I just couldn't stop myself. You looked so, I don't know, sad." Both hands on the steering wheel again, and I let out a relieved sigh. "You have a reason to be sad, I'm not saying that. But today, for some reason, I just felt like I had to see you, get through to you, you know?"

We're stopped at a red light, only four blocks from my street. Logan tilts her head, and her mouth turns down. "Please, Marsh. Can we keep talking? Can we go somewhere? Cup o'cino's, maybe?"

Coffee. Great. "Yeah," I say, shrugging away the stutter in my voice. "That would be great."

She exhales a sigh and smiles. She likes me. It's crazy. Why does this girl like me? I lean my head against the window. The glass is cold on my face. If I still believed in thin spaces, I'd be praying for one to be here. Inside this car. What I wouldn't give to be sucked out of my life right now.

Cup o'cino's is warm, crowded. A lot of kids meet here after school, but of course, lately, I haven't been one of them. I scan the menu board while Logan sways next to me. She keeps bumping into my side.

"Let's get the usual," she says. Before I can say anything, she chirps right up. "Two large caramel lattes."

I fumble for money, ignoring the driver's license as I flip through—didn't I mean to take that out yesterday, tuck it away in a drawer? Somehow a couple of twenty-dollar bills are folded up in one of the wallet pockets. I hand one to the clerk, get my change, and then follow Logan over to a table in the corner.

"Remember how we came here for that all-night study session?" she says. "And we drank so many lattes that our hands were shaking?" She leans across the table so our heads are almost touching.

I pull back, take a sip of coffee, and try not to shriek at how hot the damn thing is.

"And that night when you bought me that giant heart cookie. We sat right here at this table." I can't figure out how her voice manages to come out both high and breathy at the same time. "You were so sweet, having them write our names on it in that pink swirly frosting. And then that day—"

She's launches into another story, another coffee shop memory. I'm getting the gist of where this is going, but I have no idea what to do about it. Logan is a nice girl. I don't want to hurt her. But it's clear, to me, at least, that we're not going to be able to pick up where things left off last August.

"You had that foam mustache, and you were walking around like you didn't know, and . . ."

I grab my cup to give my hands something to do. Take a sip, try to ignore the fact that a layer of skin's been scalded off the roof of my mouth.

"—that time you built the tower out of milk containers and the owner took a picture." She hops up, dances over to the counter. "Wow! It's still there, Marsh. Look!"

I do. It is. A face that doesn't look anything like mine smiles at me from behind the milk container creation.

I head back to my seat and study my coffee cup. There's a little saying written on the side. "The truth shall set you free." What the hell is this, some kind of conspiracy?

I know I have to do it. Tell Logan what she thinks we had is over, that things—that *I'm* different now. Courage, though, it isn't one of my stronger qualities.

She plops down next to me now and her ponytail whips my face. I can smell her shampoo. Some kind of fruit scent.

"Remember when we drove up to the lake and it was so dark you could see, like, every star?"

Her voice flutters over me, and I make myself nod. Because I do remember that night. It was the four of us. My brother. Kate. Me. Logan. It must've been end of July, right before football practice started, I'm thinking now. He drove and I was a little pissed off about it. But then I didn't care anymore because I could sit in the back seat with her. Kiss her. We didn't mind either, that they were in the front seat. It was kind of crazy, how caught up we could get in each other. Like all you can think about are your hands on her and her hands on you.

Logan's right how we could see the stars that night. Ten miles out of town and it's like another world. The girls spread out a blanket in the grass and we curled up on it, joking about how squished we were. Once, I turned my head and checked out what my brother was doing. He lifted up a little and we grinned at each other. He wasn't thinking about the stars either. And then she was pressing her lips against my neck.

"I'm sorry," Logan says, and I jerk my face toward her. "I shouldn't have brought that up, that night, because he—you probably don't want to think about—"

"No, I mean, yeah." I take a glug of coffee. Somehow it's still burning my throat skin. "So," I say, because a thought occurs to me, "you ever see Kate anymore?"

Logan sighs. "Not really. She's kind of . . . I don't know."

I do know. Even lost in my fog, I've caught glimpses of Kate stumbling around the school hallways. And now I know she's been out there haunting the accident site too. The love of her life is dead. Without meaning to, I let out a strangled moan.

"I know. I feel horrible for her," Logan says. "She's a wreck. Have you seen her? She's like a skeleton." She purses her lips together. "I tried to talk to her. I mean, she was my best friend. I didn't just drop her. But she's the one who won't talk to me, you know?"

I nod and swallow more coffee. I can't even feel the inside of my mouth anymore.

"I get it. She lost him, and then she looks at us, and she's probably, like, sick about it." Logan shakes her head and her fruity hair odor swirls around me. "I know it's not the same thing, but I miss Austin too. Remember how we were the love square? The four of us?" She presses closer, grabs both of my hands. "And you and me, Marsh. Are we—do you still—"

"Logan," I say. She's squeezing my hands and her hair is making me dizzy and I can't look at her. I've got my face turned toward my coffee cup, the stupid saying about truth blurring in front of my eyes. The only thing I can manage is, "I don't know."

She drops my hands, shrinks away like I've slapped her. And then I just sit there while she's hunched over, sucking in her breath, fighting off tears. It's like my mother in the kitchen yesterday. I should say something. Do something. I don't think hugging her is the right thing though. Honest to God, I don't know what the right thing is. Truth, though—I sure as hell know it isn't that.

Truth means telling Logan I don't like her. That I don't want her telling me funny stories about cookies or coffee or milk containers. Truth means something else too—something that I can't even say to myself, let alone to Logan.

I tell myself it's okay to pat her on the back. It's the least I can do. So I do that, and I count to twenty before dropping my hand.

We don't talk on the drive home. We both stare straight ahead. I'm thinking about reality and how much it sucks. Logan's thinking about who knows what.

Me, probably, and what an ass I am.

12
More Freaking Reality

Logan's cell rings, a snippet from some lame love song. She rummages in her purse, flips open her phone. "Okay," she snaps. "I'll be home soon. Right." She rolls her eyes. "My mother. She wants me to pick up a couple things at the grocery. Do you mind if we stop there before I drop you off?"

I shake my head. "No problem." The car screeches, skids a little when she turns into the parking lot.

She circles around, frowning, then wedges the car into a space about halfway down the center row. Arctic wind whips inside when she opens the door. "Wow, that's cold," she says. "Just stay in here. I'll be back in a minute."

Before I can say okay, she slams the door. I sink into my seat. I don't know if I can feel any worse about my life. It was a stupid idea to go out with Logan today. I can see that now.

But it's reality, which is what I have to keep reminding myself. I lean my head against the seat, stare out the window.

Mucky snow crisscrosses the parking lot. I shift around, kick at my backpack on the floor between my legs. I've got too much junk in my head. I start ticking it off. The reality of homework. The reality of grieving girlfriends. The reality of lacrosse players who want to kick my ass. The reality of—

I press closer to the window, squint through the glass. Am I seeing what I think I'm seeing?

About ten yards away, a girl is pacing back and forth in front of the store entrance. I glance up at the Goodfoods sign and back down at the girl. I take in the blond ponytail, the thin jacket. When she turns her head and starts sliding in the other direction, I see a flash of pink face. Maddie.

What the hell is she—

And then I'm opening the car door and clomping through the crust of dirty snow. I see her boots clutched in her hand, and my heart starts hammering in my chest.

"Maddie," I call out.

She stops dragging her feet, scowls, and goes back to sliding.

"What are you—stop! Put your boots back on." She pushes past me. I can't keep my eyes off her feet. They blaze up red, half-covered in snow chunks.

People tromp by us with their groceries. Some of them look our way. I grab her shoulders. "Maddie, come on. What are you doing?"

"What does it look like?" She tries to shrug me away.

But I've got the flimsy material of her jacket bunched up in my hand. I can feel her shivering. I tear my coat off, wrap it around her shoulders. "Put your boots on." I try to say it in a nice way. "It's freezing out here." I grab the boots and squat down in front of her. She clutches my shoulders and lets me push a boot onto her foot. "How'd you get here? Did you walk?"

She sniffs. "Yeah."

"You didn't walk here barefoot, I hope. You took your boots off when you got here, right?"

"What do you care?" she says.

I sigh. Some guy walks out through the glass doors. He passes by, grins at us. Who knows why?

"Nothing happened." She swipes her nose with the back of her hand. "I stepped over this whole section of the parking lot."

"Well, you knew it was a long shot, right?" I pick up her other foot. It's ice in my hands. I try to be careful stuffing it into the boot. I know what that feels like, the burning skin. "Your feet, Maddie," I say, shaking my head. "Can you even feel them? You're going to get frostbite."

She sniffs again. "You didn't worry about that."

"Because I was an idiot." I stand up. The wind's whipping at us. I tug at the corners of the coat I've draped around her, try to cover up her neck better.

"So you quit looking?" she says. "That's it? You're giving up?"

"Yeah. Pretty much." I stuff my hand in my jeans pocket, find a crumpled napkin from the coffee place. I hand it to her and look away while she blows her nose.

"Why?"

"Because I'm sick of it. Okay? I'm tired."

"But you still believe," she says in a small voice. "You still believe in thin spaces." Her cheeks are streaked with sleet. It's so freaking cold out here I think any minute she's going to have tracks of ice on her face.

"No. I don't know. Look," I tell her, "I've been doing this for too long. Two months. Since Mrs. Hansel died. Yesterday, in your house, I really thought it was going to happen." I suck in my breath. "But Mrs. Hansel got it wrong. She must not have come through in front of the fireplace like she thought. So that's it. Reality. I get it. Whether there are thin spaces floating around somewhere out here or not, it doesn't matter. I'm never going to find one. It's over."

Maddie's eyes scrunch up and for a second I think she's going to start crying, but then she rallies. "But your brother," she says. "Austin."

My stomach clenches.

"Well, I want to find one." She juts out her chin. "I'm going to keep looking."

"Jeez," I say, and against my better judgment, I have to ask her, "why?"

"You're not the only person who lost someone, you know. There's someone I—"

Then she's reaching for me and somehow I'm reaching for her. We've got our arms wrapped around each other when Logan comes out of the store.

I let go, take a step back. "Logan, uh," I clear my throat, "this is Maddie…" I can't remember Maddie's last name. Which shouldn't be too surprising. It's hitting me that I don't know a hell of a lot else about Maddie either.

Logan pulls her shoulders back, makes her mouth stretch into a halfway believable looking smile. "Wow, hi," she says.

"I'm Logan Gleeson, Marsh's"—she pauses for a beat—"I was going to say girlfriend, but I guess I don't know anymore. Marsh—if you haven't figured it out yet, Maddie—is very confused lately."

"Logan," I start, but then I let it go, because it's too cold out here to get into a big discussion about it. "Could you, uh, give Maddie a ride home? She lives a few houses down from me."

"No problem." Logan marches toward her car, swinging her grocery bag like she wants to whap someone—me, most likely.

Maddie climbs into the backseat. I get into the front and push the seat up so she'll have more legroom, ignoring the fact that my knees are knocking into my chin.

"Wow," Logan says, back to using her chirpy voice. "You just moved here, right? From Nashville? So what do you think of Andover?"

"Oh, it's nice," Maddie says.

Out of the corner of my eye, I see Logan flashing her white teeth. "That's really cute. Your accent. Nice." She draws out the word, trying to say it like Maddie does.

I stare out the window at the gray sky and the mud spattered snow clumps on the side of the road while Logan keeps up her interrogation.

"You're Sam's little sister. He's in a few of my classes. Seems like a cool guy."

"Yeah," Maddie says.

"So, why'd you move here? Any special reason?"

I hear Maddie shifting around behind me. "My mother's job."

Logan's turned onto our street, thank God. "The gray house," I tell her. "Where Mrs. Hansel used to live."

"The old lady?" Logan says. She slides around, barely missing a snowdrift at the end of the driveway. "The lady you used to help every Saturday?"

"Yeah." I heave myself out of the car, knock the seat forward so Maddie can get out.

"Thanks for the ride," she says. She shakes out of my coat, hands it to me without looking. "Bye, y'all."

I watch her trudge up the walk, her shoulders hunched over, her ponytail drooping against her neck.

"Cute girl," Logan says. "That little accent of hers. If you like that kind of thing."

The wind lashes my face.

"Hey, didn't that old lady die?"

"Yeah. September." I climb back into the car, slam the door.

"Wasn't she kind of crazy? I remember you saying—"

"I never said that." My voice is loud in this cramped space. "Can you drop me off now?"

A minute later, we're in front of my house.

"Marsh," she says. "Look. I'm sorry I pushed you again. I shouldn't have—"

"Don't worry about it."

"Maybe later, when you're ready, we can . . .?" She's struggling with the question and I'm struggling with the answer.

I clear my throat but my words still come out thick. "I can't do this, Logan." And I'm out of the car without looking back.

I head upstairs and dump my books onto the bed, grab the book closest to me—trig—and dig in. Convoluted equations are easier to deal with than anything else.

I can't think about my other issues. Maddie tromping around the supermarket parking lot barefoot. What just happened with Logan. I might as well throw Kate in here for the hell of it. Three girls I've managed to hurt recently—and I'm not even sure how it happened. Okay, Logan's deluded, but she has good reasons, which do essentially lead back to me. And Maddie, the mistake there was opening my big mouth, telling her about thin spaces, not realizing she'd believe me. Kate, I don't want to get into. Anyway, if I'm trying to face reality, I've got a more pressing concern. Homework.

I don't even notice my mother until she sinks down at the bottom of the bed. "Dinner will be ready in about thirty minutes," she says.

"Okay." I tug my English book out of the pile, flip open to the story we're supposed to read.

"I fixed spare ribs," my mother says. She's looking like she wants to say something else.

What kinds of conversations did I use to have with her? We must have talked before. I must have done more than grunt out one-word answers. I try to remember something, anything. But all I can pull up are times when my brother was there too.

"You like those, right? Spare ribs?"

"Yeah. Sounds great."

"Marsh." My mother squeezes my leg. "I was thinking maybe it's time to pack up some of those . . . mementos and maybe some of his other . . . things too." She tilts her head back, squints at the ceiling. I look up too and for a few seconds I guess we're both lost in my brother's rocket ship poster.

I turn back to my book. Watch the sentences stretch across the page until they're just black lines.

"Would you be okay with that? If your father and I went through some of that stuff?"

"That stuff?" I drag a finger over one of the lines. I can't see words anymore.

"I'm not saying we'd pack up everything. You could see if there's anything you'd like to keep."

"I don't know," I hear myself say. My English notebook is on my lap. It's open to a mostly blank page, except for one word scrawled across it: *Truth*. It's like it's mocking me.

"Only if you're ready. There's no rush."

I don't know what my face looks like, but she hugs me. "It's okay, Marsh. We can talk about it later."

After she leaves, I slump against the wall, blink up at the rocket ship poster again. Then for a change of pace, I study his bookshelf. The books are in alphabetical order, something I never noticed until I started sleeping in here. I don't know why it would surprise me. He was very organized. All of his clothes hang neatly in the closet. No stray papers on his desk, just his computer, phone charger, an alarm clock. Nothing shoved under the bed except a pair of slippers.

For three months, I have worn his clothes. I set his alarm clock. I make his bed. I don't like to think about why the hell I'm doing this. It's a way to be closer to him is what I tell myself. But the truth is it reminds me what I've done, forces me to remember how much of a complete and total mess-up I am.

On that happy note, I return to my English book. The story doesn't make sense, but somehow I manage to answer all the questions at the end of the section.

When my father calls me down for dinner, I stop on the landing, poke my head into my old room. It's frozen too, stuck the way I left it in August. In the dark I can make out the piles on my desk and the dresser—the mementos my mother wants to pack away. Half-deflated balloons, dead flowers, mud spattered stuffed animals. A blown-up picture and the word *Austin* looping around the face. A glance at my clothes draped over the desk chair, a balled up sock, the rumpled bedcovers.

I can almost see my old self now, stepping out, ready for the double date with Kate and Logan. I was so smiley, so sure.

I wish I could go back in time. I wish I could smack that stupid grin right off my face.

13
Trouble

Another morning. I don't even know what day it is. Friday? When I pass Mrs. Hansel's house, I get the familiar urge to smash a window, but it's a thought that's easy to push away. Even when I believed in thin spaces, I was too much of a coward to ever do something like that.

At the bus stop, Lindsay and Heather are deep in conversation.

"I bumped into him in the hall. And he looked at me."

"Get out."

"No, I'm serious. He totally knows who I am."

"Oh, hey Marsh."

I offer the girls a polite nod. This is easy too. The version of myself that existed in August never did much more than that with Lindsay and Heather.

School. I pass Mrs. Golden, who squints at me through her office window. She's probably wondering what's on my agenda for today. Fights? Frostbite? I feel like I should salute her, kick up my legs so she'll be sure to notice my boots. *Hey, Mrs. Golden,* I want to yell. *Reality. I get it now.*

First period. I copy hieroglyphic-like equations off the whiteboard.

Second period. Class discussion about a battle. I can't figure out which war we're on, but I nod along at what I hope are the appropriate moments.

Third: pop quiz. I fill in all the blanks. Write *Marsh Windsor* next to the word *Name* on the top of the paper and am surprised to feel only a twinge of self-disgust.

Lunch, I clomp toward my usual seat. I'm really not looking for Maddie, but when I pass the lacrosse table, I catch a glimpse of her drooping over her lunch tray. Sam's hovering close, his face just a muted red today. I glance back to see if Maddie's wearing shoes. She is, her designer boots. So that's good. Brad's at the other end of the table, his bottom lip almost back to normal. I get the feeling that any minute he's going to come charging across the room at me.

I sit with my back toward him, face the wall, eat my tuna on whole wheat and try not to think about it. If it happens, what am I going to do? Try to get in a good punch, I guess, or just zone out and let him go at me.

Someone drifts through the lunch line doorway, and I brace myself for Logan. But lucky guy that I am today, it's Kate. She's wearing an oversized black hoodie that hangs on her like a garbage bag. We lock eyes for half a second then she whips her head to the side.

Hey, Kate, I hear you. I don't want to look at you either.

"Marsh," she whispers. Her knuckles are white against her tray. "I'm sorry about—I need to stop doing—I need to get—" She looks like she might keel over.

Against my better judgment, I stand, lift the tray out of her hands. She's got only three items on it: a little plastic container of fruit cocktail, a spoon, and a cup of ice. She crumples into the seat across from me. We look past each other for a few minutes. I try to swallow some sandwich.

Then she bursts into tears.

Oh, for God's sake.

"I know," she says. Whatever that means. She keeps sniveling, dragging the sleeve of her baggy sweatshirt across her face.

A part of me wants to shake her, scream in her face. A bigger part just wants to disappear. But manners and common decency seem to require something else. "Hey," I say, pushing my napkin toward her.

She crushes it in her hand, blinks at me for a second, and then falls back to crying.

I've done my share of crying. Once, in the hospital as I watched my father sign my discharge papers. Once, here at school, my first day back after the accident, the first time I ran into Kate over by the lockers. Of course Logan was right there too. Because back then the two of them were practically joined at the hip.

I twitch around in my seat, catch Logan's eye over at the football groupie table. Heave out a sigh then force myself to look at Kate.

She's fiddling with her fruit cup. She doesn't eat, just twirls her plastic spoon around, pulling up fruit chunks and dropping them back into the syrupy gloop.

I've lost my appetite too. Now that I'm face to face with her, only a foot away, I feel my stomach lurching, my head pounding. This is worse than drinking scalding coffee while Logan babbles on about the good old days.

"You know the other day." Kate bunches the napkin against her nose. "At the corner. When we talked?"

"Yeah," I say. But I don't think I can handle whatever she's going to say next.

"When I saw you . . . walking across the street, with your hands in your pockets . . . your head was back and your hair was off your forehead." She sniffles out a sobby snort. "You looked like him."

Nice, Kate. Thanks! We looked alike. We were freaking interchangeable. I get it.

She's crying like we're the only two people in the cafeteria. We're tucked away at this corner table, but I can sense the audience behind me, stretching, shifting, gearing up for the next scene in the crazy saga of the remaining Windsor brother.

"I know I'm being stupid." She lifts her head and her face is so blotchy and pathetic-looking I can't help wincing. "Because you're not him. I know that. And I have to get over it."

"Kate," I say. I can feel my teeth grinding together.

"But he was the love—"

Please don't say it.

"—of my life."

And now I remember why I hate her. Don't lose it, I tell myself. She's no worse than anyone else.

But that's the problem. She's *not* anyone else.

First day back at school, when I came limping around the corner, brace on my leg, gruesome scars tracking across my forehead, I don't know what I'd hoped she'd do. Run toward me. Wrap her arms around me. It was a one-second fantasy. That she'd lift her head. That she'd look at me.

Instead, she and Logan blubbered with each other against the locker. Crying *Austin* over and over. I was an idiot to imagine any other scenario. What happened with her and my brother—that erased everything after. I'd dated Kate for a long time. I thought I loved her. She thought she loved me.

Funny thing. We were both wrong. End of story. Reality 101.

I stuff my half-eaten tuna sandwich into my lunch bag. Kate's back to stirring her fruit lumps. Her cup of ice is mostly melted.

"I saw you in Mrs. Golden's office," she says. "She's been calling me down there a lot too."

Probably a good idea since she's obviously got some grieving issues. "Yeah, well," I say.

"I guess we have a lot in common. We both lost—" The sentence breaks apart.

And somehow I'm falling backward.

I can't breathe. I push my hands out reflexively, try to grab something but catch only air. My legs kick out too, my booted feet thudding against the underside of the table. Something's squeezing my neck. It releases for a second, and I gasp, "What the—?" before my throat closes up again.

Kate's a smudge of black, and then I don't see her anymore. I'm on my back, but not on the floor. Someone's under me. I throw my hands out, clutch at the arm against my neck. Jab my elbow backward again and again.

I hear a grunt. The arm releases and I suck in a deep breath. I squirm away, twist around, and swing. It's Brad. We roll together. My face hits something wet. Fruit cocktail, I'm guessing, and then I taste blood. It must be mine because pain is shooting through my nose. I've felt that pain before. When my face hit the steering wheel.

Now Brad's got me pinned down with his knee. His fist blurs as it slams into my chin. I've got one hand gripping his shoulder and then I let go. I let him hit me. *Good*, I think. *Smash it. I can't stand looking at my face anymore.*

There's a rush of air. Hands pull him up, off me. I see Chuck, Kate, the cafeteria ceiling. And then I'm surprised to see Maddie leaning over me. Her ponytail is loose and hair's falling over one shoulder. Her face is pale. She disappears when other hands seize my shoulders, heaving me to my feet.

Mrs. Golden's office is now my home away from home. I'm parked in my usual chair, in front of her cluttered desk. There's the folded up towel. She must be holding on to it in case I decide to tromp around barefoot again. There's the picture of her and the smiling old guy. Probably her husband. Now that I think about it, he's dead. So I guess we do have something in common. I look up, check the ceiling, searching out the fungus blotch. It's bigger today, spreading onto the surrounding tiles. Pipe leak, maybe, or snow buildup on the roof.

Brad's kicked out next to me. He's got an icepack on his eye. So I must've landed a couple of decent punches after all.

I've got my own icepack. My nose throbs from the cold but I keep pressing it down, ignoring the icy burn.

It's just the two of us in here at the moment. Mrs. Golden left to round up Mr. O'Donnell and our parents. When we got hauled in, she shook her head at me, muttered "Oh, Marsh," a couple of times, and pulled the icepacks out of the little refrigerator she's got behind her desk.

I should be stressed, but for some reason I'm relieved. My conversation with Kate is effectively over. Brad most likely got whatever he needed to out of his system. And I've got a rearranged face for a few days. If I get sent home from school, that's just an added bonus.

I hear Brad shifting around. "I hate you," he says in a grunty voice. "I've hated you since seventh grade."

Against my better judgment, I look at him. "Why?"

He lifts the icepack away from his face. His eye's swollen shut, bluing around the edges. His lips have that fish-mouth thing going on again. "You don't know?"

I shrug and pain shoots through my shoulder. "I guess not."

"You're an asshole," he says.

"That's my line." I try to laugh but my nose feels like it's going to split open.

"You knew I liked her and you went after her."

"Her?"

"Courtney."

"Courtney?" I don't know who the hell we're talking about.

"Courtney Johnson. Football cheerleader. Remember, she moved away summer before eighth grade?" Brad's swollen eyeball is so disgusting that I jerk away from him, sending a fresh surge of pain through my shoulder.

"You're mad at me because of some crap that happened in middle school?"

"You knew," he says.

"Come on. This is about Courtney?"

"Man, you're doing the same thing with Logan, stringing her along." He shifts his head to glare at me, which truly must hurt him, because he moans. "Cut her loose. Stop torturing her."

I sigh. "You've got it all wrong." Why am I having this conversation?

Brad clutches his icepack, shakes it at me, comes narrowly close to clipping me on the chin with it. "You think you get a free pass, Marsh?" he says.

I clear my throat, ignoring the spasm in my nasal cavity. "What?"

"Because you lost someone, you think you get to do whatever the hell you want?"

"Look. You don't know what you're talking about."

He puffs out his bloated lips. "You get to shit all over people. You get to—"

But I never get to hear what else I get to do because the door opens, and Mrs. Golden strolls in to start the suspension meeting.

She pushes some chairs around in a circle and everyone has a seat except Mr. O'Donnell. He stands with his hands on his hips and gets the ball rolling with a lecture on the school fighting policy. Brad and I have the same idea with our ice packs—we keep them over our faces so we don't have to look at anyone. The glimpse I do get of my parents makes me want to crawl under Mrs. Golden's desk.

"The rules are very clear—"

What the hell was I thinking before? About relief?

"Previous physical altercation Wednesday—"

My mother's hands shake in her lap. My father clutches his tie.

"The four-day suspension will—"

My brother's gone. I've destroyed my parents. And jeez, Brad, do you really think I'm getting a freaking free pass here?

"Mr. and Mrs. Silverman," Mr. O'Donnell says, and Brad's parents rise. Brad stumbles to his feet and follows his happy parents out of the room.

The icepack burns my skin, pulses toward the back of my head, it reminds me—

"Some other issues to discuss," Mrs. Golden is saying.

—how cold my feet were when I walked outside. How the icy concrete burned right through them and shot up my legs—

"About counseling."

—when I was looking for a thin space—

"Marsh."

—and any minute I might find it, step into it.

But that's over. Done.

"Marshall."

And now it's time to go. My parents trudge out to sign my suspension papers. I follow them into the waiting room, tilt my throbbing head toward one of the grimy windows.

Sixth period now, I think. Outside, some PE class is trekking across the football field in the snow. The gym teacher leads the march, blows a whistle that I can't hear all the way up here. There's one girl hanging back at the end of the line.

I watch her stoop down. Kick off her boots.

When I feel Mrs. Golden swaying behind me, leaning toward the window, I move out of her way. *Better hold on to your dishpan,* I feel like telling her. But I say nothing, of course, and then I'm leaving the room, trailing my parents out of the building.

14
Seething

Nobody says anything when we get into the car. My father shakes his keys, coughs. My mother's rigid next to him, fiddling with her scarf. The car hasn't warmed up yet. My breath puffs out of my mouth. I'm in the backseat, still pressing the icepack against my nose, but the thing doesn't feel cold anymore.

We roll through the parking lot, pass the football field. There's the gym teacher waving his arms around. There's Maddie stooping down, stuffing her feet back into her boots.

She must've been trolling around on that online obituary page she was telling me about. Maybe she read about some kid dropping dead on the football field. I could've saved her the trouble and the foot pain. Back in September, I limped the length of that field several times. No soul came through there. Maddie's wasting her time.

Whatever she's trying to do, it's my fault. I shut my eyes, see a flash of her pale face today when she leaned over me in the cafeteria. When I was sprawled out on the floor, getting pummeled by Brad, Maddie must've come over to see what was happening. Along with everyone else in the school.

I pull the icepack off, chuck it on the seat next to me.

"Oh, Marsh," my mother says. She keeps her head faced forward. "You broke your nose. Don, do you think he broke his nose?"

"It's just bruised." My father keeps his eyes straight ahead too. It's like they're having a conversation with the windshield.

"Maybe we should take him to the doctor's to check. It could've damaged the same place."

"There's nothing to do for a broken nose." The light turns yellow and my father slows the car, stops. Suddenly I feel like crying. It's my Dad. How freaking cautious he is.

"What are we going to do?" my mother says.

"Helen," my Dad says in this crushed, beaten down voice.

I snatch the icepack up and put it on my face so I won't have to keep looking at them. There's only a dull pain now, pulsing out, radiating across my cheekbones. But that seems to be the extent of the damage.

This is nothing compared to after the accident. The first time the nurse showed me a mirror, I couldn't stop staring at my face. The eyes sunk into the swollen skin. The nose bulged out, twisted to the side. The forehead and chin, split apart and blotchy—purple, black, yellow. *Marsh*, my mother wailing over and over until I thought I was going to lose my mind.

Wait, I told her, the mirror shaking in my hand.

Marsh—

Wait. I mean, what the hell is going on?

Before I can stop it, there's a spark of anger. My mother's sniffling into her scarf. My father's switching on his turn signal, looking dutifully in both directions before turning. And I'm sitting here in the backseat, seething.

It starts in my feet, rises into my throbbing chest. My hands curl into fists around my useless icepack. It pounds in my jaw, my head. It has nowhere else to go.

"We need to talk," my mother says, "Marsh."

"Stop." I grit my teeth, and the movement sends a jolt of pain through my nose. "Please, Mom, just stop."

"Don't you dare use that tone with your mother," my father snaps. "Do you understand how serious this is? You've been suspended. For four days."

"I know, Dad." I press harder on my icepack. I feel like jamming it into my skull.

"We're trying to understand, honey," my mother says. "Did that boy provoke you? Were you defending yourself?"

My father exhales a sigh. "That kid's face was in worse shape than Marsh's."

"I'm just saying that if he had to fight back, I can . . . understand."

My entire head is pulsing. I can hear it—the blood surging through the veins around my eyeballs.

"Violence isn't the answer. We taught our boys—" His voice cracks. "We taught Marsh better than that."

"It's not his fault," my mother says sharply. "There are extenuating circumstances. That's what Linda Golden said.

He needs help. What we're doing, what we've tried to do—it isn't helping him."

"So what *are* we supposed to do? What?" My father's voice cracks again. There's no way I can handle him crying. "Tell me, Helen. What's the answer here?"

I'm gripping the icepack so hard now I think it might split apart.

My mother turns to look at me. There's a sharp intake of breath at the sight of my face. Then she slumps forward and I can hear her soft moaning.

"Mom," I croak out. I can't say anything else.

It's never going away. This reality. I can see that. What I did back in August—that set something in motion, something that can't be stopped.

My father puts the blinker on even though we're just turning into the driveway and there's no other car on this street. I shove my way out, suck in a breath of icy air, head into the house before I can say anything—do anything—worse to my parents.

—*m*—

They ground me. Not that it really matters. I have nowhere to go. First day of my suspension, Monday, I shut myself in his bedroom. If I hear my mother saying *Oh, Marsh* again, I might slam my fist through a wall.

She took the day off from work. I can hear her puttering around downstairs. Clattering dishes in the sink. Vacuuming. Once when I emerge to take a shower, I pass my room. I see she's picked up, removed the balled up sock from the floor and the clothes that were draped over the desk chair. There's a couple empty boxes on the bed, ready and waiting to be filled.

Just looking at them makes my head pound.

Day two, I plow through all my schoolwork. Suspension technically means you get a bunch of zeroes for everything you miss, but the school is kind enough to let me make things up. Probably Mrs. Golden's doing. Whatever. The work keeps my mind busy.

Day three, I can't stop looking at my face in the mirror. My nose bulges out. A strange array of colors spreads across my cheeks. For the moment, I look like someone else.

Later, my parents take me to my therapy appointment. It's one of the things the school suggested, that I get back into counseling. I know there's no way it's going to help, but I act like I'll try it.

When we walk into the clinic, I have a major blast of déjà vu. Over three months have passed by, and here I am back in the same place. I've looped right around to where I started.

The counselor's one of those ageless-looking guys. He could be thirty or sixty with his short blond hair, wire glasses, and loosened tie. I sink down in the same overstuffed chair I sat in the last time I was here. I notice he's still got a tissue box prominently displayed in the center of the glass coffee table.

We shake hands, scroll through the initial small talk: *how are you, good to see you.* He plunks down across from me. "So, what's the other guy's face look like?" he says.

Ha ha. The guy's such a jokester. Then he gets down to business, more déjà vu about opening up, expressing myself, letting it all out. Apparently, it's his standard lecture.

I nod along. Because it's good advice. Theoretically.

Now he's channeling Mrs. Golden, exploring the guilt angle. "It was an accident," he says. "It wasn't your fault."

More nodding from me, even though the movement reminds me that I have a bashed-in nose.

"Did you feel connected to your brother? Did you feel like you were two halves of the same person? Because I've read that about twins, identical twins, especially. That they have a bond that goes beyond the normal sibling..."

I fade out here and start thinking about Brad for some reason. What is it like to be Brad? To have no identical Ben or Bill wearing the same face? To be just a lone, solitary guy? People see you and meet you and talk to you, and you're just Brad, the guy they meet, the guy they know.

What's that like to never have someone blink at you and wonder who you are?

"—difficulty in moving beyond a loss," the counselor is saying.

Because that's what it was like for me and my brother every single day of our lives—people pausing and frowning. *Marsh?* they'd say. *Whoops! I mean Austin, sorry.* The teachers wrinkling their foreheads: *Twins, how cute. Now, which one of you is which?* Our friends, laughing, *MarshandAustin,* running the words together so it was one name, and they wouldn't have to take a guess.

"—coping with the loss of a part of yourself—"

Who wouldn't get tired of that? Who wouldn't wish for one second that you could have people know you for *you*? Without that stupid pause, that intake of breath, while they thought, *Is it him, or is it the other one*?

"—learning to face a reality that includes only one—"

Honest to God, it was one second, one freaking second, that I wished it.

"Marsh," the counselor says.

I can feel the vein pulsing in my head, my teeth grinding together. I grab the tissue box to give my hands something to do.

"I'm doing all the talking here." Laugh. "It's your turn now. Do you have something to say?"

"Uh. Not really." I clear my throat. "Unless you have a time machine stashed somewhere in your office."

Another laugh. "What I mean is that opening yourself up, letting things out—this can really—"

How many whack jobs have sat in this overstuffed chair and listened to this guy drone? Did any of them feel like crushing a tissue box? Did anyone ever want to bang his head through the glass coffee table?

I imagine that gruesome scenario for a minute, and it's strangely enjoyable, then before I know it, my mind's traveling down a familiar road.

Let's say a guy couldn't take any more of this blah blah express yourself crap. So he killed himself—took himself out of the world, right here, in this overstuffed chair. Unbeknownst to him, his mother once sat in the same space. She was messed up too, maybe worried about being pregnant, who knows. So she was sitting here like, twenty years before, at the moment her baby's soul came through.

Which made a thin space in this shrink's office. Right here, where I'm sitting, pulverizing a tissue box.

I'm probably going to rip the damn thing to shreds. I can feel my fingers scraping against the cardboard, the tug in my knuckles as I pull. It's like I'm possessed. *Stupid,* I tell myself. *You* are *alone now. You got what you wanted.*

I chuck the tissue box down and my mind goes blank. Suddenly I find myself bending forward, reaching for my bootlaces. The movement is familiar, comforting, right. I'm slipping out of my boots, yanking off my socks.

I stand up. Press down.

It's a long shot. A wild goose chase. A needle in a haystack. The chances that the same guy came through and went out—

Remote, I know.

But Mrs. Hansel—that day in her front room, when she looked at me . . . Even on her last day on earth, when she was about to pass through herself, she lifted her hand, pointed it right at me. She knew.

I'll make a thin space. That's what she told me. *You can see your brother.*

And I have to believe her.

15
Break

Day four of my suspension, Thursday afternoon, and I'm waiting outside for Maddie. My parents are at work. Left me home alone with milk and sandwich meat in the fridge, a load of laundry to do, and trash to haul out to the curb. They've given up talking to me, and they're barely speaking to each other. I know they're losing it, floundering around with their own sadness and anger.

"Grief takes time," the counselor said after I followed him out of his office, barefoot, swinging my brother's boots by the laces. My parents stared at my feet, at each other, and at the counselor. He shrugged his shoulders. "Grief takes time."

He's wrong. A ticking clock isn't going to change anything. The truth is I set this mess in motion and there is no other way to fix it.

Gray-white day. The clouds are swollen with a storm. According to the weather channel, a cold front's supposed to barrel through tonight. Tomorrow, Andover will be the arctic tundra.

The bus rumbles up to the corner, and I hang back, leaning against a pillar on my front porch. Lindsay and Heather step off first, huddle together before hiking off in the other direction.

Then Maddie stumbles down the bus stairs, her face down against the wind. I head across my yard toward her, tromping over the packed snow. "Hey," I call out.

"Marsh," she says, and my stomach twitches.

But I try to sound light, friendly. "I guess you know I got suspended. Today's my last day."

She nods. We're standing at the foot of her driveway, facing each other. We both look down for a second. I'm checking to see if she's wearing her boots—she is—and maybe she's wondering the same about me—I am.

"I was waiting for you," I say. The wind pushes between us like a wall. "I need to talk to you."

Maddie turns toward her house. "You can't come in," she says.

"I know. Your brother, he doesn't—"

"No," she says, "*I* don't want you to."

I probably deserve that. The past few days I've been thinking about Maddie. When I stuffed her feet into her boots in the Goodfoods parking lot. When she trooped around the football field. When I saw her leaning over me in the cafeteria.

"I have to ask you something," I say. But I stop because I'm not sure how to phrase it. The thing I've been thinking about is this: What made Maddie cross the cafeteria that day? Was she just like every other face in the crowd, curious to watch a fight? Or did she want to see *me*?

I clear my throat. "Uh, when I got in that fight with Brad—"

"Brad's a dumb jerk," she says. "I'm not doing that carpool anymore." She lowers her eyes, shudders. "Your face looks . . . really bad."

"It's just bruises. I've had worse."

"Well, I'm glad you're okay."

"Yeah, I'm fine. Really. I hardly notice it." I stare at her cheeks, how the red spreads out across her skin, and suddenly I know it. She did want to see me. She was worried. I'm feeling like this is an important point, but I'm not exactly sure why.

"Good." She glances toward her house. "So, what'd you want to ask me?"

I switch gears here, because I don't want to talk about the fight anymore. "I've been thinking about your idea, the obituaries you found online. I saw you on the football field last week, and I figured you must've read something on that site about it. Did a person die out there?"

"Yeah. A long time ago." She juts out her chin. "You know what? I'm really cold. I'm going inside." She starts to push past me.

"Wait. Are you mad about something?"

"Marsh," she says, drawling out the word and sending another twitch to my stomach. "The last time we talked your . . . um . . . girlfriend was giving me a ride home."

"Logan's not my—"

She puts her hand up. "And the time before that, you told me you were using me to get inside my house."

"I never said—"

"Plan A, to get into the front room of my house. That's what you told me."

"I wasn't using—"

"Whatever. It's okay. I don't care."

"I didn't mean . . . It's not what it . . . Really. I wasn't—" I know I'm babbling like an idiot. I can't remember where I was going with this. Talk to Maddie after school—that was the extent of my plan. "Listen. I'm sorry." But she's marching away, the wind whipping her ponytail. "Wait! You're right."

She flips her head around.

"It's crazy, I know." My words rush out before I can stop them. "It's like I've been in a fog. Since I woke up in the hospital, and I found out about my brother . . . See, everything's so messed up." Big understatement of the year and I laugh a maniacal-sounding laugh.

"What?" she says.

"You're right. I guess I was sorta using you. Which is not cool."

She frowns. "It's not."

We stare at each other. Maddie's wearing that same worthless jacket. Her ponytail is flicking around in the wind. Someone needs to buy her a hat or something. "I'm sorry," I say again.

The frown's still there, then her eyes widen and she smiles. "Hey," she says, "did you ever try walking barefoot around a cemetery?"

"No"—I smile too—"because people don't die in cemeteries. They're just buried there."

"Huh," she says. "You're right."

"Look," I say, and it's like the last time I unloaded on her. I'm half-relieved just to get what I'm thinking out of my head. "I know I told you I was done with it. There's no thin space in your house. So, okay. Mrs. Hansel didn't make one there like she thought she would, but the thing is, there's got to be thin spaces out here somewhere. Maybe I'm crazy. Maybe I just don't want to think about—" I stop because I realize that my body is shaking—my legs, my hands, my teeth. Like chills when your body is fighting a fever.

"What?" Maddie's voice is quiet. "What don't you want to think about?"

The wind lashes tears out of my eyes. It's truly amazing how cold it is out here. "My brother and I, we did this stupid thing. We—well, really, it was *me*. Last summer *I* did this stupid thing. See, I—" The truth is on the tip of my tongue, but I'm not sure I can say it. I'm not even sure I can think it. "The truth is—" I suck in my breath and it's like I'm gasping for air. "I just have to see him."

"So what are you going to do?" she says.

"I don't know. I was kind of hoping you'd have an idea."

"I've been thinking about it." Maddie wraps her arms around herself.

"Come on," I tell her. "Let's go inside before we freeze to death."

"I'm not sure—"

I cut her off. "It's okay. We'll go to my house."

The last time a girl sat in my kitchen was August, the double date from hell. My brother and I ordered a couple of pizzas. Faster and a little cheaper, we thought, than going out to dinner. We were both nervous that night. The girls, of course, had no clue. The four of us sat around the table, right here, where Maddie and I are sitting now.

"It happened in the nineteen fifties," Maddie is saying. "A quarterback named Robert Hinton got tackled on the twenty-yard line and he never got up. It didn't seem like he'd been hit that hard, so it was this big, shocking thing. The obituary went on and on about how the whole town showed up at his funeral."

"Maybe he had a heart problem," I say. I pour Maddie a glass of milk, drop a bunch of cookies onto a plate, and set it on the table. I'm feeling kind of rusty about my hosting skills. I notice that Maddie's sitting in the same chair Logan sat in that night.

"That's kind of scary," Maddie says, taking a bite of cookie. "You could walk around with a defective heart and never know it. Anyway, I stepped over the twenty-yard line and nothing happened. Maybe I was off a little, or maybe he didn't die exactly on the line."

"It doesn't matter," I tell her. "I already tried it. I walked the whole field back in September. What else have you got?"

"A kid passed out in a science class. That was in nineteen seventy-six. He had a seizure."

"Really?" I raise my eyebrows.

"Yeah, but he didn't die until a few days later in the hospital. So that one's out."

She's still nibbling the same cookie, while I'm popping them in my mouth whole, one after another, something my brother used to do too. One thing we had in common—our appetite. That night, nervous as we were, we wolfed down the majority of the pizza.

"So." I clear my throat. "Is that it for school deaths?"

Maddie laughs then covers her mouth. "I shouldn't laugh. It's just kind of a weird thing to talk about. But yeah, no one else died at Andover High as far as I can tell." She tugs her jacket off, folds it over the back of her chair. "It's so warm in your house. Our house is crazy cold."

"Oh yeah?" I say, grabbing the last cookie off the plate. "I thought someone came over to fix your furnace." I'm trying to stay present in this conversation, but as usual I'm having a hard time with it.

"The same maintenance guy's been out three times already, and my mother's freaking out because it's so expensive, and it's still not working—"

The funny thing was how easy it turned out to be. The trick, I realized, was to ignore both girls. Shrug away the breath tickling my ear and the arms draped around my brother. If I just concentrated on the pizza, I was okay. Every once in a while, though, I'd catch what they were doing, and I'd want to punch him.

"—I've got a pile of blankets on my bed, and I have to wear socks. I hate that, wearing socks —"

Twenty minutes of pizza and I just wanted to get the hell out of the house. Get the stupid date over with. We were halfway out the back door when my parents got home. Neither one of them gave us a second look. Just my mother calling out *Drive careful* and that was the end of it.

"Marsh." Maddie's waving a hand in front of my face. "You're zoning out on me."

"Oh. Uh. Sorry."

"You know you do that a lot."

"I think I might do that with everyone."

"So"—she tilts her head to the side—"I shouldn't take it personally?"

I nod.

"I'm sorry too."

"Why?" I see another flash of Kate and Logan in the kitchen. Red fingernails trail my brother's cheeks, flutter over his smirky face, and I have to shake my head to push the memory away.

"I feel bad," Maddie says quietly. "About what happened to you. It's awful. I mean, what I heard about the accident . . ." Her voice trails off.

Another flicker of the pizza boxes yawning on the table, of my brother. The black T-shirt he wore that he'd borrowed from me.

I grind my teeth, force myself to focus on Maddie. Her pink face, her ponytail, the strands of hair coming loose from her hair tie.

"It seems like a really hard thing to get over," she says. "To live with."

"Yeah." I stare at the half-eaten cookie in Maddie's fingers, her sweatshirt, the sleeves tugged up, baring her pale arms.

When I sense the red fingernails and black shirt starting to shimmer again, I clear my throat. "Tell me what else you read when you were doing your research."

Maddie opens her mouth, and I notice that her two front teeth overlap a little. "It goes back to the druids," she says. "Only priests were allowed to step in thin spaces. When they did, they believed they were standing in both worlds at the same time. Ours and the other world, the spiritual world."

"I don't remember Mrs. Hansel saying anything about druids." For the moment, surprisingly, I'm still here, with Maddie, in the kitchen. "Did you read anything about how to find one?"

"No. Their thin spaces were always outside, though, under old trees or near a cave or a spring. The druids would sort of mark off the area with stones."

"Stones?" I think of those pebbles Mrs. Hansel had scattered all over her house.

"And later, people built churches on those sites because they were considered sacred."

"Yeah, so that doesn't help us."

Maddie smiles. "Unless we want to go to Ireland."

Out of the corner of my eye, I can see them laughing, kissing.

"And I couldn't find anything about *making* thin spaces. I scrolled through a lot of stuff, and there's nothing. A lot of it's just speculation anyway. There aren't many written records from that time period."

I notice Maddie's still rolling half a cookie around in her hand. "Are you going to eat that?" She shakes her head and pushes it across the table toward me. It's not even good, one of those organic brands my mother is nuts over, but I take my time chewing it. It keeps me here in the present moment.

"Plan B," I say, and I have to clear my throat. "It's almost impossible."

Maddie shrugs. "But what else are we going to do?"

I like how she says *we*.

16
Plan B

Apparently, last summer, a guy collapsed playing tennis at the park in our neighborhood.

"Yeah, but did he come through in the same space?" I ask Maddie. It's funny how you forget how cold it is and the minute you step outside you remember. Wind blasts our faces as soon as we open my front door.

"Probably not," Maddie admits. "But who knows. His mother might've strolled across the tennis court. Or maybe the courts weren't built back then, and she just went for a walk in the park one day."

We hurry down the dark street. Snow's already swirling down. We race with our heads bowed, tilted toward each other.

"You've got to get another jacket," I say.

"I know," she says. "My mother keeps saying she'll take me shopping but she's so stressed lately. Her new job, moving..."

I peel off my coat, and she waves her arm. "What about you, though?"

"Don't worry about it." I stop, glance over my shoulder. We're already halfway there. No time to turn back. Technically, I'm still grounded, and Sam doesn't want Maddie hanging around with me. So we have to be fast. Get to the park and get home before anyone figures out we're gone.

The sweatshirt I'm wearing does nothing to block the cold. And why didn't I throw on a hat? At least I thought to bring a towel. I've got it folded up under my arm. We can use it later, to wipe off our feet.

"So when we get there," Maddie says, panting, "I'll start on one end, and you go to the other side and we'll meet in the middle."

"There are two courts out there," I say. "Maybe three."

She groans. "The article didn't say which court the guy died on."

We're running full out now, down the center of the street. I grab Maddie's elbow to keep her from slipping.

I have a one second flash of my brother and me riding our bikes down the same street, those early morning workouts during football, but I brush away the memory and focus on clutching Maddie's arm.

The park's deserted, of course. No one else is crazy enough to be outside on a night like this. A couple of streetlights flicker over the tennis courts. Maddie races ahead of me toward the chain-link fence.

"It's unlocked," she says. I can hardly hear her over the wind. She bends down, starts pulling off a boot.

"Wait." I sprint toward her. "I should do it. No sense both of us freezing our feet off."

But both boots are off and she's already barreling through the gate. "That's stupid," she says. "We can do it faster this way."

I tug at my wet bootlaces. My cold fingers shake as I fiddle with the knot.

Maddie's tramping along, walking a line. "Holy moly!" she cries. "It's cold out here."

I head toward the far end of the court. Pass the nets that hang stiff and frozen over the drifting snow. Then start my own trek, skiing across the snow. The wind stings my face. It comes back to me fast, the way the icy ground stabs your bare skin, shooting right up to your knees. It's the only thing I can think about.

It doesn't take that long, but when we meet in the middle of the center court, we're both shivering. Maddie drops to the ground, throws her legs up in the air.

"I can't feel anything," she gasps.

I plunk down beside her, cradle her feet in the towel.

"Oh, oh," she keeps saying, and she's half laughing. "This is crazy, isn't it?"

"Insane." I slide one foot into her boot, still holding the towel around the other one.

"Thanks," she says. "That's better. Let me do you."

She's gentle, but my feet still burn and throb in her hands.

Boots back on, we stand up, look at each other. "I guess the guy's soul didn't come through on the tennis courts," Maddie says.

"It was a long shot." But the funny thing is, I don't feel that horrible about it. "Got any other ideas?"

She nods. A gust of wind smacks her ponytail against her face and she swipes it away. "I've got a list."

"Really?"

"A homeless guy died outside the bus station downtown three weeks ago. Two people passed away at a convalescent home. An old woman died in her house. That's probably not a good lead though. I'm not breaking into someone's house." She shakes her head. I notice her teeth are chattering. "The best bet is the hospital. Most people who die in Andover die there."

"Hmm," I say. I'm not thrilled about going back to the hospital. But maybe if Maddie is with me . . . "Yeah, I guess we could try that, the hospital."

I hold her elbow as we tramp out of the park. I'm thinking about nothing except my boots against the snow, my numb fingers around Maddie's sleeve.

When we reach her driveway, she shrugs out of my coat. "Well, that was . . . fun." She flashes me a smile, then sprints across her yard. I watch her stamp her feet on Mrs. Hansel's welcome mat and disappear into her house before I turn against the wind and head home.

⁓

My parents have to accompany me to school the next morning, the first day after my suspension. Really, only one of them has to come with me to sign me back in, but it's a serious situation, they tell me, so they've both decided to go. We drive past the bus stop and I catch a glimpse of Lindsay and Heather, hitched to each other like a two-headed girl, and Maddie, swaying a little off to the side. Still not dressed for this weather, I notice, in that flimsy jacket.

Mrs. Golden's waiting for us in her office. I only half listen to her spiel. "Hope you had time to think . . . completed your assignments . . . accept responsibility . . . get along with your fellow . . ."

Yeah, yeah, yeah, whatever. I'm just glad it's Friday.

My parents fill out some forms. My mother gives me an awkward hug. My father chucks me on the shoulder, not looking at my face. When they finally leave, I take a step toward the door, but Mrs. Golden stops me.

"Marsh," she says. "There's something else I want to talk to you about if you don't mind." She motions toward my usual chair and I sink down in it.

She sits down at her desk. One hand's over the other on the desk blotter, and she's fiddling with her diamond ring.

I tilt my head back and check out the status of the ceiling fungus. It's inching across five tiles today and looking a little furry. When is the school going to take care of that?

"I've noticed something interesting," she says. "You know the family who moved into Rosie Hansel's house?"

I keep my head back, my eyes focused on the mold blotch.

"Madison Rogers, she's a sophomore here. I think you might know her."

"Yeah, I do." My mind's reeling. Where's she going with this? Something about Brad and the fight? Is she thinking it had to do with Maddie? Or did she overhear Sam griping about me and his sister?

"Interesting," Mrs. Golden says again.

I force myself to lean forward, look at Mrs. Golden's face. Her eyes are hidden behind the glare of her glasses.

"Did you know that the PE teacher caught Madison Rogers walking around barefoot?"

Uh-oh. I shift around in my chair.

"Outside," she continues. "The other day that girl took her boots off and ran around barefoot on the football field."

What am I supposed to say here?

"Marsh"—Mrs. Golden stands up, walks around her desk, sways over me—"do you have any idea why she would do something like that?"

There truly is no answer to this question that will satisfy Mrs. Golden.

"Is this a weird . . . club you're starting? Some kind of polar bear thing?"

I blink at her. "Polar bear?"

"Listen to me. I've talked to Mr. O'Donnell and to your parents too. We've made a decision. No more. We're not going to tolerate it—the bare feet. Do you understand?"

"Uh, okay, I—"

She cuts me off. "And we sympathize. We do. I do. I've told you before that we—the teachers, Mr. O'Donnell, and I—are sorry for your loss and we want to help you in any way we can as you work through your grief. But there are some things that we just can't condone." She bobs her yellow head. "You are going to wear your shoes in this building and on school grounds from now on." She pauses, looks down at my boots, then back up at my face. "And whatever is going on between you and Madison Rogers, you can pass this information on to her too. Do you understand what I'm saying?"

<center>~~~</center>

I don't see Maddie until the end of the day. No lunch together, we decided, to make it easier on Sam. It's not me, Maddie keeps saying, he'd be that way with any boy, but I have my doubts. I don't want to push the guy. I don't need more complications in my life right now. And protective older brothers clearly fall into that category.

"I've got a weird message to give you," I say as we head toward the bus. "From Mrs. Golden."

"Now what?" She rolls her eyes.

"What do you mean?"

"Every time we turn around, she's, like, there. She's been to our house every day practically since we moved in. Just wants to see how we're settling in, she keeps saying. Yesterday, she gave us a plant, a giant fern that probably won't last two seconds in the meat locker we call home." She laughs.

I laugh too. Then stop because it's sort of pathetic. "Maybe she's lonely. I don't know. She probably misses Mrs. Hansel." I shake my head. "They were pretty close."

I give her the quick rundown of Mrs. Golden's warning.

"Polar bear club," she says. "That's funny. But who cares? We're done with the school, right? No thin spaces there." She

149

presses a folded up piece of paper into my hands. "My list"—she lowers her voice—"of possible thin spaces."

We sit down in the back of the bus, and I flip open the paper. It's a chart listing the places Maddie told me about the day before: convalescent home, bus station, hospital. Across the top, she's written *Plan B*. The first entry, tennis court, has an *x* marked next to it.

"This should keep us busy," I say.

The bus jerks forward, knocking her into me. She grabs my arm and her face flushes. "Sorry," she mumbles, letting go quickly.

"So"—I clear my throat—"where should we start?"

The coast is clear for both of us that afternoon—all parents working late and Sam off with his lacrosse buddies—so we walk downtown to the bus station. This time we're more prepared for the weather. I insist that Maddie wear my coat again. I've found another coat—actually it's mine—tucked away in the closet of my room. I've also dug up an extra hat and gloves because I know Maddie doesn't own much winter gear.

We're bundled up good when we set out, and of course we're both wearing boots.

"I was an idiot before," I tell Maddie, "walking around barefoot, thinking I'd find some thin space by accident. No wonder everyone thinks I'm crazy."

"Not crazy," she says. "Just kind of ... messed up. But who isn't, right? I mean, look at me."

"You're not messed up," I say.

She smiles. "You don't know me, though, do you?"

We clomp on. Most people haven't shoveled their sidewalks, so we veer into the street. It's slushy there, from the salt trucks, and muddy. Even though we're dressed better, it's still unbelievably cold.

We reach the bus station and Maddie marches up to one of the glass doors, yanks it open. "I want to warm up first," she says.

The place is dead. Maybe it's always like this on Friday nights. Only a few people sit scattered around the room. We head toward an empty row of chairs, sink down across from each other, and stamp the muck off our boots.

"What do you think it will be like?" Maddie says.

"Mrs. Hansel talked about how misty it was. I always picture winter in Andover." I let out a laugh. "How gray it is here."

"It is gray," Maddie says. "Kind of depressing."

"I bet you miss Nashville."

"Not really." She tugs off her boots, wiggles her toes. "But I meant, what do you think it will be like when you see him—your brother?"

"Oh." His face floats in front of me like a balloon. Funny thing, this is the first time I've thought of him today.

"You think it's going to help you?" The hat I've lent her swallows up her head so I can't see her hair.

I stand up, nod. Hell yeah, it's going to help me. I'm counting on it. But all I say is, "Come on. Let's do this, fast."

Carrying our boots, we push through the glass doors, pace up and down the snowy sidewalk. I don't think I'll ever get used to the cold, the stab of the icy concrete against my skin. We don't talk, just walk a line back and forth, trying to cover the whole area as fast as we can. A few people heading into the bus station stare and shake their heads at us, but nobody says anything.

I stomp along, shuddering, imagining that homeless guy clutching his heart, falling out on the sidewalk. What a crappy way to leave the world—in front of the grimy windows of a bus station.

But he didn't come through here. We know that after only a few minutes. Another space to cross off the list.

I'm okay about it, though, when we head home. I know we've got more places left to try.

It's not until later, when I'm sprawled out on my brother's bed, staring at his rocket poster, that I remember Maddie's question again.

Here's something that hits me. Who does she want to find in the thin space? And what help is she hoping for?

17
Tricks and Lies

On Saturday we decide to try the convalescent home. Maddie found out that the place was built in the 1960s. Before that it was farmland. Andover's the type of town where people live their whole lives. Generations of the same families lived and died here. Some of these people's souls might've come through and gone out in the same space.

Still, I'm not feeling too optimistic about our chances of finding that space at the Green Lawn Convalescent Home.

"I'm not sure about this," I say when I meet Maddie outside her house in the morning. "I keep picturing the thin space as something you have to step into. If there's a building on the space where there didn't use to be one, maybe it won't work right."

Maddie arches an eyebrow. "But you don't know that."

True, I have to admit.

She starts hurling questions at me. "How wide is a thin space? How tall? Does it have mass? Volume?"

"I don't know," I answer her over and over. *I don't know.*

We're trekking down the center of the road again, toward downtown and the bus station. There's a complicated bus route that'll get us out to Green Lawn—Maddie's got the whole trip planned—it involves three bus changes and at least an hour, and that's just getting out to the place.

It would be easier to drive, of course, but I flip that thought right out of my head. No. Not doing it. And I'm grateful that Maddie hasn't even suggested it.

It's colder today, if that's possible, but for some reason the sun flickers at us between clumps of gray clouds. It shocks me every time it happens. Sun in Andover, in November? What? Is this the end of the world?

Maddie's not finished with her interrogation. "Is a thin space like an elevator? Will we step on it and get whisked up or down? And why do you have to be barefoot? That part doesn't make sense." She stops, frowns. "What's so funny?"

"Nothing. Just, you sound like my brother. He asked Mrs. Hansel stuff like that too." I shrug. "He was the logical one in the family."

"Hmm," she says. "What did she tell him?"

"She didn't know how it worked exactly—the technical part of it—just that it did." My boots tromp through slush. Maddie's probably right. It's weird. It's impossible if you really think about it. But I've become a master lately of not thinking about stuff too deeply. "Mrs. Hansel believed it," I say. "How she talked about—that story she told, about when she was a little girl—maybe if you'd heard her—"

"I'm not saying I don't believe you. I'm just trying to understand."

"I know." I feel the image slithering through, Mrs. Hansel sunk into the pillows. It's the moment I keep coming back to, the moment that gives me hope. But how can I explain this to Maddie? I don't even understand it myself.

She's quiet on the bus home. We found nothing at the convalescent home, which, to tell the truth, doesn't shock me, but I'm trying not to dwell on it.

"You're a genius," I say. "Telling the receptionist we wanted to gather oral histories of Andover. How'd you come up with that?"

She tugs my thick hat off her head, smooths her hair. "I was just trying to think of a way to get inside the rooms."

"Well, it was inspiring."

"It was a lie. We tricked them."

"Nah," I say, waving a hand. "Those old people liked talking to us. You could tell."

"That's what I mean." Her hair's all static-y and she pats at it, but since she's wearing gloves, it just makes it fly out more. "They thought we really wanted to know their stories. But we didn't."

"Yeah," I say. "But *they* didn't know that."

"That doesn't make it okay. It was wrong. We shouldn't have done it."

Why do I feel like I've had this conversation before? The bus lurches forward. The jerky movement, the odor of gas and smoke—and I remember. My head clenches up and I try to let it go. I lean back in my seat, close my eyes, but the stupid memory slams into me anyway.

Logan was curled up next to me. "Put your seatbelt on," I snapped. I felt her flinch but I kept my eyes straight ahead. I didn't know what my brother and Kate were doing in the backseat. I didn't want to know. *What the hell?* I kept thinking, the whole time getting more and more pissed off.

The second we dumped the girls off, I tore into him, "How could you?"

He just shrugged, smirked. "Well, that went well."

If I hadn't been driving, if I didn't have to keep my hands on the wheel, I would've—

"Marsh?" Maddie's patting my knee with her gloved hand. "Are you okay?"

I nod, try to adjust my face so I don't look deranged.

"Zoning out on me again," she says.

"Sorry about that." I try to concentrate on Maddie's gloves—my gloves, on her hands. They're way too big for her and dangle around her wrists. She's still tapping my knee. "So what's next on our list?"

She pulls one of her gloves off, gets the list out of her jeans pocket. "The hospital. But that's going to take more time."

And more lies, I think as I get a flicker of my brother's glaring face. He tells me to let him out. He yells, *When are you going to get over it?* He unbuckles his seatbelt—

I have to stop reliving this.

"Maddie." I say her name slowly, try to anchor myself to the present. "You never told me. Who do you want to see in the thin space?"

She doesn't answer. The bus lumbers into downtown Andover, stops on the corner of Main Street. Maddie pushes the hat back onto her head, clasps the collar of her coat tight against her neck. I follow her down the bus aisle, out onto the frigid street.

"Who?" I say. Maybe she doesn't want to tell me. Usually I'm not the type of guy who would force something like this, but I can't help it.

She blinks up at me. "My father."

"Oh." I don't know why this surprises me. I know her mother is a single parent, but I remember her saying something about a divorce. Everything else is kind of hazy. Probably because she's right: a lot of the time, I have been zoning out on her.

"That story Mrs. Hansel told you," she says, and her breath puffs out around her mouth, "about her father dying when she was a little girl—it's kind of the same for me. After my father died, things got kind of messed up for my family too."

"Oh," I say again. I'm not good with these kinds of conversations. What are you supposed to say? Nothing really. Of all people, I know that. When someone dies, there's not much you can say that's going to make a difference. The situation seems to call for something, though. So I fall back on one of the lines people liked to throw at me after the accident. "I'm sorry, uh, for your loss."

She sighs. "It's not that big a deal. He died when I was six. I hardly remember him."

"How'd he die?"

157

"Cancer. It was a long, drawn-out thing. Half my life, it seemed like he was sick."

"Sorry," I mumble again, and I sort of get why people say it. Maybe it's just a way of telling a person, *Hey, I hear you.* Which is kind of ironic, now that I think about it—because I really haven't been listening to Maddie all that much.

We hike together down the center of the street, past the movie theater, and I pointedly ignore it. The sky's a big smudge of gray dumped out over us. No sign at all of the sun. Maybe I hallucinated it this morning.

"Do you think that's stupid?" Maddie says. The hat droops over her eyes and she nudges it up. "Wanting to see someone you didn't really know?"

"You must've known him a little," I say.

"Not really. If I didn't have any pictures of him, I don't know if I'd remember anything. And sometimes I think it's just the pictures I remember and not real memories." Her voice is so low I have to lean closer to hear her. "I have this one picture where he's helping me button up my coat. I can see his fingers on the buttons, you know, and his face bending toward me. He had this very pronounced Adam's apple and a pointed chin. But here's the thing—that's all in the picture. So do I really remember him or am I just imagining I do?"

"It sounds like a real memory," I tell her.

"Maybe." But it doesn't sound like she believes me.

When we hit the turnoff into our neighborhood, I realize I don't want Maddie to stop talking. I think it's her soft, drawling voice. Or maybe it's just that she's talking about something that has nothing to do with me.

158

"So, what else do you remember?" I ask her.

"I don't know. I've heard a lot of stuff about him—stories from Sam, because he remembers a little more than I do, but it's not the same thing as knowing a person yourself. And it bugs me, how I'll never be able to know him myself."

"But he knew you."

She lifts her head. "Do you think so?"

"Well, yeah. He was your father." My voice comes out louder than I mean for it to. "He'd know you."

This is probably a lie, though. Because lately it's pretty clear to me that people don't know each other as well as they think they do.

She's staring at me. For a minute I think she's going to start crying, and I try to mentally prepare myself for it. Instead, her mouth slips into a half smile. "That's what I've been hoping."

We trek past Mrs. Golden's house. I shoot a glance at her front windows, half expecting to see her pouf-ball yellow head plastered to the glass. Then we veer into Maddie's driveway and she pulls off the hat and gloves.

"Maddie," I say, because I'm still not ready for her to leave me. "You said before that things were kind of messed up after your father died."

One arm's out of her coat and she stops. "Yeah. It's a long story."

"I have time," I say. I clutch the coat, helping her back into it.

"Well." She hesitates for a few seconds then sighs. "After my father died, my mother remarried two more times. Sam and I, we never really liked those guys, and my mother, she was like Mrs. Hansel's mother. Not really . . . involved with us anymore. I think that's why Sam's the way he is, you know? Because he feels sort of responsible for me . . ."

"Which explains why he doesn't want you hanging around the school lunatic," I say, winking at her. "Right?"

Maddie grins. "Actually, he thinks *I'm* the lunatic. At least since we moved here. I've been having these horrible dreams. Every night practically, I wake up and think someone's in my room." She shudders. "Talk about crazy, right? Maybe it's the house. It's like it's haunted or something. It gives me the creeps. Ever since I found out Mrs. Hansel died there."

"I guess that's my fault."

She shakes her head. "No. It was Mrs. Golden. Remember? She told us about it the day we moved in. That night I woke up and there was a man in my room. It was so real. I mean he was just standing there at the foot of my bed. I screamed and Sam freaked out. He came running in with his lacrosse stick. He thought someone had broken in. But it was nothing. Just a nightmare."

"Jeez, nightmares," I say because I'm not sure what the proper response is.

"Yeah, and every night it's a different person. A man kneeling. This old white-haired lady." She stutters out a laugh. "Sam thinks I'm losing my mind. It's probably why he's in such a cruddy mood. Because of me, waking him up every night."

She takes off my coat, presses it over my arm. "So there I go again, talking your ear off. Half the time you're not even listening, but whatever. That's okay."

"No," I tell her, and this is a truthful statement, "I am listening." Today at least. But I don't tell her that part.

She hands me my hat and gloves. "That's pretty much my messed up life story, I guess. Now you know everything. If you want to run away screaming, I'll understand."

"You're the one who'd run away screaming," I tell her, "if you knew my messed up story."

"Marsh," she says, drawling out the word, "whatever you think you've done that's so terrible, it's probably way worse in your head than in reality."

I let out a snort. Because wouldn't that be nice if it were true? I want to say something else to her. *Thank you*, maybe, because I can't remember the last time I had a few hours like this, where I'm just me, and there's no anger or guilt or disgust. But two things happen right then that put an end to that sentiment.

One, Mrs. Golden glides across the street holding a cake.

And two, Sam bursts out the front door.

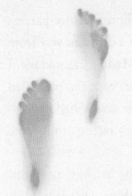

18
Fun at the Hospital

They both start talking at once.

"Madison, what's going on?" says Sam.

"I thought you'd like to try my German chocolate cake. It's an old family recipe," says Mrs. Golden. "Is this a bad time? Should I come back later?"

"We were just out walking," Maddie says quickly. The arctic wind blasting our faces makes that statement seem absurd. Especially now that Maddie's not even wearing a coat.

"My heavens, it's cold out here." Mrs. Golden squints at me, bobs her head. "Hello there, Marsh. It's nice to see our little talk the other day . . . has resonated." I'm getting the distinct impression she's checking out Maddie's and my feet. Satisfied, that we aren't totally nuts, she turns to Sam. "Is your mother at home? I would love to say hello to her."

"Yeah. Uh. Sure," he says. He glowers at me, and Maddie gives me a little wave then darts across the yard.

When I get home, I'm relieved to find that my parents aren't there. My head's spinning, but in a different way from normal. It's churning with things that Maddie has told me. I can picture it, like a movie in my head. A younger, pig-tailed version of Maddie. A man buttoning her coat. Shadowy figures swaying at the foot of her bed. Sam racing around the cold house swinging his lacrosse stick.

I shed my winter gear, plunk it in the hallway, and head upstairs, tired suddenly, as more of Maddie swirls around in my mind.

I must've fallen asleep. The room is dark, shadowy, when I jolt awake. I blink at the rocket ship on the ceiling, the swirl of smoke puffing out behind it. I'm stiff, bleary-eyed when I climb out of bed. My mind's still pulsing with the day. The convalescent home. The bus. But mostly I see Maddie. Her gloved hands waving around as she talked. My wool hat pushed down on her head.

We're walking around the hospital tomorrow. That's the plan anyway, unless Sam decides to have a conniption about it. But I don't let myself go there. Maddie's a determined person. At least she seems like that to me. If anything, she's just as into finding a thin space as I am.

I pad down the hall, rubbing my eyes. No idea what time it is or if anyone's home. I stop outside my old room, peer inside out of habit, and my heart sputters because someone's lying on my bed. I get a creepy flash of Maddie's nightmares—of people breaking into her room—before I realize it's my mother.

She's on her side, curved around a couple of open boxes, eyes closed. Even in the dark I can see her body shaking.

She's got something bunched up in her hands, and I can't help it, I take a step into the room.

She twitches, blinks. "Marsh?" she says.

I see what's in her hands now. One of those stupid blown-up photos. I can just make out an eye, half a lip, the looped letters: *AUS*. My mother pulls herself up, perches unsteadily at the edge of the bed and a box tips off, clunks to the floor.

"I came in to straighten up," she whispers. "The things from the accident—I can't look at them anymore." She shakes the picture, and it's like she's waving a flag of surrender. "I'm sorry. I don't like for you to see me like this."

I'm stuck, one foot in the hallway and one foot in the shadowy bedroom. A wild thought flips around in my head. It's me, crossing the room, grabbing my mother by the shoulders. Telling her what I've done.

Once and for all, just letting it out. Truth, like the dumb saying on the coffee house cup. The truth shall set you free or whatever.

"Don't pack up everything," I manage to croak out. "Can you wait a little longer?" I keep my mouth open, try to say more. I can almost see myself doing it, spitting out the rest of what's crammed up in my head. But I can't imagine what would happen after that. What my mother's face would look like. Horror? Anger? Shock? Her son, the person she thinks she knows—

Something rumbles up from my chest. It's a laugh, and I quickly swallow it down. Maybe I'm going to crack. Have a delayed nervous breakdown. It almost happened in the hospital the day I found out he was dead. When my parents stood by my bed, moaning *Marsh* over and over, that's when I should've said it. I should've hurled myself out of that freaking bed and screamed at them.

But is this something a person can even say to his parents?

I get a flash of Maddie when she talked about her father, wanting him to know her. I've got news for her. He probably won't.

I grab the doorway to steady myself. I can't keep doing this. It's pointless—stupid—to keep replaying it. I suck in my breath, squeeze my eyes shut, will the anger to leak away.

When it's all gone, my mother's just a sad lump on the bed, clinging to a crumpled picture. "I won't," she says, her voice cracking. "I mean, I'll wait, Marsh."

I sigh as I help my mother up, walk with her across the room. We part ways in the hall—my mother heading downstairs, mumbling about ordering a pizza, and me, back to brother's bedroom where I'll stare at his ceiling until our dinner gets delivered.

―――

Maddie and I are standing in the hospital lobby when she starts a new line of questioning. "What about your story?" she says. "I spilled my guts to you yesterday. Now it's your turn."

I don't know what my face must look like, but Maddie's cheeks immediately fire up. "You don't have to tell me if you don't want to," she says. "I was just thinking that I don't know a lot about you." She raises an eyebrow. "Besides your interesting choice of footwear. Or lack thereof."

"Well . . . uh . . ." I really do want to talk to her, it's just that what I want to talk about is *her*, not me. To buy a little time and throw her off track, I point to the hospital gift shop. "Let's buy flowers first."

"Okay," she says, but she picks out a clump of *Get Well Soon* balloons instead. "This is better than flowers. People will be so focused on these they won't notice our bare feet."

I have to give her credit here. She's very thorough. The more time I spend with her and her Plan B chart, the more ridiculous I feel about my old method: shuffling around aimlessly.

We head over to the elevators, the balloons bobbing along behind us.

"How'd you get past Sam's eagle eye today?" I ask her. "*That's* the story I want to hear."

She groans. "I told him I was hanging out with Lindsay and Heather."

"He bought that?"

"It's not a total lie. They invited me to a movie. I'm meeting them at the theater at four o'clock."

"Fun," I say. "Lindsay and Heather."

"I know." She smiles. "But they've been kind of nice to me. Probably because Lindsay has a crush on Sam, but that's okay. I haven't made that many friends yet. . . ."

"Yeah, sure. That's cool."

A balloon thumps my chin and Maddie yanks it away. "I don't know if I should warn her. He'll never go for her. She's a sophomore, so too young, according to him. It's one of the main reasons he hates *us* hanging around."

"Right," I say, even though I highly doubt this.

Maddie must doubt this too, because she makes a snorty sound. "Okay, you've got . . . *issues*, he says. Like we all don't. Whatever. It didn't help that my mother was there too, with Mrs. Golden and her dumb cake."

"Jeez. What did *she* say?"

"She was all like, 'this is off the record. I'm not being a guidance counselor, I'm being a neighbor.' I thought any second she was going to bring up how I walked around barefoot on the football field. She stared at my feet the whole time she was talking—"

"About me," I say, because I have a feeling that's where this is going.

"Yeah." She looks at me, and then quickly averts her eyes. "She said you were going through a rough time. And she started talking about your brother. How he was a great kid— how both of y'all were smart and athletic, the popular guys in school. She really went on about it, how wonderful everybody thought you were."

"Huh." I let out a breath. "You're embarrassing me." But for some reason, this conversation isn't pushing me over the edge. Maddie's looking up at me expectantly, so I smile. "And Sam's *still* not thrilled about me hanging out with you?"

"Well . . ." She bites her lip. "That was the good stuff. Mrs. Golden had other things to say too."

Balloons whack me in the head when we step on the elevator. I knock at them so the doors will close.

"Which floors did you do last time you were here?" Maddie says.

I shrug. "I don't know. That day's kind of blurry to me now."

She pushes the button for the top floor, keeps tapping at it even though the light's already on. "If you want me to stop talking about this, I will."

"No, keep going," I tell her. I feel my feet heavy on the floor and my stomach dropping as the elevator shoots up.

"So then she said that your barefoot fixation—that's what she called it—was upsetting to people because it was like you didn't care about yourself anymore. And she brought up what's been going on with Brad, and Sam had to put in his two cents about that. How that just proves you're unstable. I tried to tell them it wasn't your fault. You didn't even start those fights."

"Which I'm sure your mother believed." I say it like I don't care one way or another, but it feels kind of nice to know Maddie's defending me.

The elevator squeaks to a stop. The doors ding open, and we step out into a fairly busy hallway. There's a waiting room immediately to our left and we move toward it.

"My mother," she says, stopping for a moment to look at the TV bolted to the wall. It's blaring some news channel even though the waiting room is empty. "She's kind of ... in her own world lately. You know, she actually made a joke to Mrs. Golden about my stupid nightmares. Can you believe it? I thought I was going to die right there."

The conversation's off me, so I let out my breath. "Did she give you a good dream analysis? Mrs. Golden lives for stuff like that."

"No." Maddie frowns. "All she kept asking was who the people in the dreams were, did I know them. I mean, what difference does that make? It was weird."

I nod. "Yup, that's our friendly neighborhood guidance counselor. Sometimes she gets weird ideas stuck in her head." Inside, though, I'm thinking of her staring me down in her office, making me say the accident wasn't my fault. But no point going off on that depressing tangent.

"Oh, and listen to this: out of the blue, my mother has to bring up her divorces—plural—and my father dying. It was like 'spill the family drama' day at the Rogers' house. Sam left all mad, then my mother and Mrs. Golden and I ate some of her cake. She got kind of upset after that. Did you know her husband died of a heart attack a few years ago?"

I scratch my chin. "That's right." I don't know why I've forgotten this. "He was out shoveling, I think."

"That's horrible," Maddie says. "Lots of death in our neighborhood." She blushes and throws her hand up to her mouth. "Oh. I'm sorry!"

"It's okay," I tell her. "I don't mind talking about it with you." I say it to make her feel better, but it's halfway true. "You didn't know my brother. Everybody else around here, that's all they're thinking when they see me—my brother and me and the accident. But you—all you know is me. Crazy barefoot guy at the bus stop."

"Hey." She sounds offended. "I never thought of you as crazy. I'm here with you now, right?" she drawls the word. "We're fixing to slide around a hospital looking for a doorway out of this world." She laughs.

"True," I say, and I have to laugh too. "Well, let's go find it."

I think I could do this all day—tiptoe around corners, slip into empty rooms, pull off my shoes, and sweep the floors with my feet. For some reason, Maddie and I can't stop laughing. She makes up this system where one of us checks if the coast is clear and the other covers the area. We do little chunks like that all day, stepping in and out of our shoes. Maybe it's the balloons. They keep whacking us. Or maybe it's the weird looks we get from the people in the halls. I feel like I'm a kid, playing a game that's not allowed. And it just makes me crack up more.

When we hit the ward where I stayed during my recovery, I hesitate before getting off the elevator. Maddie doesn't seem to notice. She's out of breath. On the last floor, a nurse yelled at us, told us we needed to settle down and get to where we were going. Maddie and I grinned at each other. "Yeah, we're trying to get sucked into the afterworld," I whispered, and she practically lost it.

But being back here doesn't bother me too much. No one looks familiar. The hallways themselves don't seem different from any other hallways in the building, same hospital smells and noises. I can't even remember what room I was in. The whole time I was here is kind of foggy. It was only the day they discharged me that I started to feel like myself. That was when I watched my father sign the papers and I looked at my face in the mirror. That was when a lot of stuff hit me, about the accident and before.

And that was when I wished I could crawl back into the fog.

"Marsh?"

Funny thing, maybe I'm still trying to do that. Step into a thin space, escape into fog.

"Marsh? Are you okay?"

A balloon taps the side of my head and I blink down at Maddie.

"You zoned out on me again," she says.

"Sorry." I keep my eyes on the clump of balloons. One of them looks like it's lost most of its helium. It's just sitting on the floor jogging a little up and down. "Do you really think this is going to work?"

"I don't know." She bites her lip. "Do you want to quit?"

It's not like it's a difficult question, but for some reason I can't think of a response.

"Marsh," she says in her soft, twangy voice. And just like that, I know what my answer is.

"No," I say. "I'm not quitting."

The two of us cover a ton of ground, but we're nowhere near finished. Too many occupied rooms. Too many suspicious people walking the halls. At three-fifteen, we've got to stop. We need to catch the bus downtown so Maddie can meet Lindsay and Heather.

On the way over, she asks me if I want to see the movie too.

This shouldn't be a difficult question either, but the problem is the last time I went to this theater was with Kate and Logan. I'm not sure I can handle reliving that night.

"It's okay," Maddie says. "No big deal. Another time."

But when the bus lets us off downtown, I find myself following her across the street. I can't keep avoiding this place, I tell myself.

It's just a movie theater. What's the worst thing that can happen?

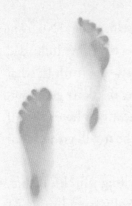

19
Showtime

"Before we go in, I have to tell you something." We're standing in line at the ticket booth, nudged up against each other because it's so freaking cold out here.

"Okay," Maddie says. "Shoot."

Without thinking about it, I start blurting it out. "See, my brother and I came here with our girlfriends one time and—"

"Kate and Logan?"

My heart heaves up into my throat. "You know about this?"

"No," she says, "but I heard that Austin used to go out with Kate, and I know about you and Logan."

"Yeah, uh, well—" I can feel my stomach roiling. "It was a double date. Last summer." I get a nice painful flash of the four of us standing on this very sidewalk. Logan's breathy voice skimming my ear. Kate worming her way practically up into my brother's armpit. The stupid smirk on his face—

Maddie curls a gloved hand around my arm and I shiver. "Is this going to be too much for you?" she says. "To be here?"

Yeah, I think, but instead I find myself saying, "No." I'm getting that weird feeling again, like other times I've unloaded stuff on Maddie, that maybe it'll be okay. The truth is, what happened that night is hanging over me. If I don't get it out, it'll knock around in my head for the next two hours. But if I can *say* it, just throw it out there, maybe it will go away for a while.

I clear my throat. "I guess I started telling you this before, about how my brother and I did this really stupid thing." I shake my head. "No. It was *me.* It was my idea, this stupid thing—"

Before I can finish, Lindsay and Heather come skipping up with their arms linked. "Maddie!" Lindsay gushes. "We were just looking for you!" Her mouth makes an O. "Whoa. Are you guys together?"

Maddie's looking up at me and I nod—because what the hell? We're standing here together, aren't we?

Lindsay and Heather pass each other knowing looks, then cut right in front of us and launch into one of their standard inane conversations.

"No way."

"I told you—"

"You did not—"

I turn back to Maddie, who's half smiling at me, her head tilted away from the girls. "So you did a stupid thing," she prompts.

I nod. "Right. My brother and I asked Logan and Kate to see a movie. Well, the four of us did that a lot, went to movies. I mean, what else is there to do around Andover? But anyway, it was summer, and we were going to this movie." I'm rambling, trying to circle back to the point, but it keeps slipping away from me until it's our turn at the ticket booth.

I scan the list of movies and realize I've heard of none of them. "What do you want to see?"

Maddie raises an eyebrow. "*Pulse Referendum.*"

"Okay." I have no idea what that is. "Two for . . . uh . . . *Pulse Referendum*?" I say, and fumble around in my pocket for my cash. There's a nice, pathetic flash of déjà vu as I skip past the driver's license, and I curse myself yet again for not getting rid of the damn thing. Glad to see there's still some money left. But why wouldn't there be? It's not like I've been a big spender. A few bus fares, cheap hospital flowers, that pretty much covers my expenses these past few months.

We push through the doors and the popcorn smell hits me. "We never ate lunch," I say to Maddie. "You want something?" We sidle over to the concessions line, notice Lindsay and Heather already swaying in it, and I consider cutting in front of them this time but decide to let it go.

I'm not done with my story, and now I'm feeling that if I don't get it out of me, I might spontaneously combust.

"You don't have to pay for everything," Maddie says. "I invited you, remember?"

I wave my hand in front of my face. "Whatever, but listen. See, that night was kind of messed up." I close my eyes for a second and it's like I'm back in the dark theater, sitting next to my brother and the girls, the light from the movie flickering over us. The sick feeling, like I'd been punched in the gut, that comes back too, so I have to stop, open my eyes, and search out Maddie's face, just to keep from hurling all over my boots. "See, that night my brother kissed my girlfriend and—"

"Wait," Maddie says, and the word has two syllables. "I thought you said *you* did something stupid."

I blink at her. I don't think I'm telling this story right.

"Marsh." It's Heather. "I don't have enough money. Can I borrow a couple dollars?"

"Yeah, Yeah," I say. I dig into my pocket again—I freaking hate this wallet!—thrust some bills at her. I'm practically doubled over when it's our turn at the counter. Maddie wants popcorn. I get a big bucket but can't imagine eating any of it. A voice is screaming in my head, *Tell her, for God's sake. Tell her.*

"My idea," I say. "Because of what happened after the football practice. See, I was coming off the field and I took off my helmet. It was really hot that day, and anyway my head was sweaty and I was exhausted, and someone came running behind me and started tickling me."

Maddie's frowning. She's probably thinking: *Where the hell is he going with this story?* But I press on. "I turned around, and it was my brother's girlfriend. I tried to laugh it off. I said to her, 'Hey, wrong guy,' but she did what people usually did when they saw one of us. She stared at me. She had to think about it, see? She had to take a minute to figure out which one of us was which, and then she apologized, of course, all embarrassed because she made a mistake." I let out a sigh. "It happened all the time. So it wasn't like it was a big surprise. But here's the thing: you think some people—your girlfriend, well, you think *she'd* be able to tell the difference, right?"

Maddie's forehead's wrinkled up. I'm only halfway through with this and my stomach gives another lurch. I'm wondering if I've made a mistake, if I should shut up. I'm holding the popcorn, and I notice that my hand's shaking. Pieces of popcorn have been dropping out, leaving a trail down the hallway.

"Marsh," Maddie says, "let me hold that."

"They filled it over the top," I say. "I don't know why they always do that."

She slips the bucket out of my hands as we walk into the dark theater. I'm surprised how crowded the place is. Sunday afternoon and it looks like half of Andover High is here. I do a quick scan of the rows and spot Chuck and my old football buddies sprawled out in the back. The lacrosse guys are up there too, apparently recreating the high school cafeteria placement. So there's Brad, of course, his legs kicked out over the seat in front of him, his arm around some girl.

Big shocker: it's Logan. They're leaned toward each other, knee-deep in conversation, so for the moment, neither one of them seems to notice Maddie and me.

I grab Maddie's elbow and guide her down front, on the side, and hope that we can stay unnoticed.

Lindsay and Heather skip past. "Why're you sitting so close to the screen?" Lindsay squeals. "We want to sit in the back."

"Go ahead," I say. "What the hell? Do what you want." Both girls back away like I'm a crazy person.

"We're going to stay here," Maddie says quietly. "I'll catch up with y'all later." Then she turns to me and lets out her breath. "Are you okay?"

I don't even know. I have to take stock of myself. I'm sitting in the theater that I vowed never to step foot in again. Half the school is sitting behind me, including a guy who wants to kick my ass and a girl who'd probably like to help him. I'm spilling my guts to Maddie, who, when I'm finished, in all likelihood will never want to look at me again. What am I leaving out? I crane my neck around, half expecting to see Kate hunched over somewhere. Instead, I see a familiar square jaw up in the lacrosse row, and I sink lower in my seat.

What the hell is so special about this movie? Pulse Resolution? Revolution?

"Sam's here," Maddie says matter-of-factly, but she scrunches down too.

"Should we try to make a break for it?" I'm getting that hysterical hurtling-toward-a-breakdown feeling, and it's pretty clear that this isn't the right time or place for it.

The theater lights dim. The previews flash. The surround sound blares on and the walls thump with noise. Around us people are still talking. Maddie whispers in my ear, "Tell me the rest of your story."

My stomach tightens up, but I open my mouth and somehow words come out. "After what happened on the football field, I told my brother we should switch places. We did that sometimes—switched places—when we were younger, at school, to play a joke on our friends, to fool the teachers. But we hadn't done it in a long time."

"Y'all really looked that much alike?" Maddie asks. I can feel her eyes roaming over my face in the flickering dark.

I sigh. "Yeah. Pretty much. We couldn't see it. I mean when I looked at him, I thought we looked different. Most of the time he *did* look different from me. He kept his hair longer." I tug at the hair curled over the top of my ear, fight the urge to yank harder. But I'm going off track. I sigh again. "Good friends could tell us apart. And our parents, of course. During football, though, when we both had short hair, people had to look closer, had to pay attention."

Okay, that's it, I think. *I'm done. I've hit my limit.* Even just talking about this is pissing me off all over again, like I'm back at football practice and the guys are going *Marsh, I mean Austin,* until I wanted to tattoo my freaking name on my forehead.

"So you switched places," Maddie whispers, "and tricked your girlfriends?"

It sounds crappy the way she says it. I suck in my breath, heave it back out. "Because I told my brother the girls didn't really know us. He didn't think it was a big deal. He said sometimes people make mistakes and that was all it was. But I said I could prove it." I swallow the knot in my throat, try to keep my voice steady. "And I did."

I don't know what I expect to happen here now that I've said it, now that the words are out of my mouth. Did I think that my head would split open? That my heart would crack apart in my chest?

Maddie's leaned against me, her ear hovering near my mouth, her ponytail brushing my nose. She turns and I can feel her breath on my cheek.

"Marsh," she says, "it was after you switched, right? That your brother kissed your girlfriend?"

"Yes," I say louder than a person should speak in a movie theater. The guy in front of us flips around, frowns, and I wave at him, lower my voice. "He kissed her. She kissed him. They kissed each other." I can't say anything else. All I see is his smirking face. And I'm shaking. My boots shudder against the grimy theater floor. My hands tremble on the armrests.

"I'm sorry," Maddie whispers, as the words *Pulse Referendum* blaze up on the screen. A few people actually hoot and clap. "Are you going to be all right?"

I don't know.

"Shh," she says. She claps her hand over mine, steadies it. "We don't have to talk about this anymore."

"No," I say. "Yes." I take a breath, feel my boots settle against the floor and my hand under hers, still now, warm, against the armrest. Miraculously, my stomach stops heaving. So maybe it was enough. What I told her. Maybe I don't have to keep going with it.

Maddie's got the popcorn bucket on her lap, and here's another miracle: I think I might be able to handle some. I grab a handful and wait for the memories that are lurking to rear up and hit me, but they don't come. Instead, I stay anchored to my seat, here with Maddie, watching *Pulse Referendum*. The few flickers I get of that other night—I push those away like puffs of popcorn.

Somehow I stay present in the darkness. Light flashes on Maddie's face. Her ponytail nudges my shoulder. Once she lets out a laugh and I look over at her surprised. Later, she gasps, and that catches me off guard too. The movie makes no sense, but I don't want it to end.

When the credits start rolling, I squint at the screen for a few seconds before I'm back to reality. The audience is talking, laughing, so I know we've got to get up too, get out of here before we're stuck in the crowd.

"Let's go," I say to Maddie. She presses her head against my shoulder, turns it slowly, and I get a wave of hair against my chin. It hits me that I've crossed some kind of line with Maddie. Messed up person that I am, I'm not sure how that happened or even what happened exactly.

"That was good," she says.

My heart thunks before I realize she's talking about the movie. "It was great," I tell her. I realize I'm definitely not talking about the movie, and I'm confused again, but there's no time to think about this. We're in the aisle, the mob surging around us. I grab Maddie's hand and weave us toward the door. My legs are stiff, but I pick up the pace as we push into the light. Reality's bearing down on me, and it's saying: *Get the hell out of here.*

Ahead is the exit sign and I tow Maddie toward it. Too late, I see it's a dead end, one of those emergency exit only doors, and when I turn back around, we're stuck in the middle of half the people I know.

Chuck reaches us first, thrusts an arm out, whacks me on the shoulder. "Marsh," he says, grinning. "I thought that was you. What are you doing here, man?"

"Some movie, huh?" I hear myself saying.

"I know. This was my third time. That one part when the guy ran into that—" He takes in Maddie next to me, and his mouth curves into a goofy smile.

Circumstances demand some kind of introduction, so I clear my throat. "This is Maddie Rogers."

"Hey," Chuck says, his goofy smile widening. "That new guy, Sam, you're his little sister?"

There's another unspoken question buried in there, something along the lines of: *Are you two together?* "Yeah," I say, and I can feel Maddie's warm hand pressing into mine.

"It's good to see you," Chuck says. "Been a while since you've been . . . out and about."

I shift back and forth, eyeing the faces spilling out of the theater, expecting Sam to come barreling toward us any minute. I crane my neck around, searching for another way out of here.

"That fight with Brad," Chuck says. "Man, that guy's such an ass. You were robbed, Marsh. Four days of suspension for what? Defending yourself?"

"Yeah." I sigh.

"But, hey, your nose is better. Brad still looks like shit. Teach him to mess around with a football player." He laughs. "Hey, some of the guys are talking about getting together, heading over to my house. You want to come?" He smacks my shoulder again.

I've forgotten how physical Chuck is. On the football field, we used to go up against each other during scrimmages. Chuck was always my one-on-one partner. We got so we could read each other, really know what the other one was thinking. Like Chuck would do this thing where he'd lean to one side, and I'd know he was faking, that he was going to shoot out the other way. And he knew my little quirks too, things I was doing that would give me away. We'd slam into each other and then laugh about it, how well we knew each other.

Funny thing though, beginning of every season when my brother cut his hair, Chuck was just like everyone else— *Marsh, I mean Austin, ha ha, whatever*—until we tackled each other on the field. Then he'd always know for sure it was me.

"Well?" he says. It's amazing that he's still talking to me, still acting like nothing happened. Like we're still friends.

"Uh, thanks for asking," I say. "But I'm going to pass on that tonight."

He nods. I get the feeling he wasn't expecting me to say yes anyway. I have this weird thought, to bend down, to lock eyes with him, say, *Hell yeah, I'll get together with you guys, and hey, Chuck, watch this*, as I stoop down and charge at him.

Lucky for him, I don't have time to mess around. Anyway, my football career's long over. I give him a little wave, then squeeze Maddie's hand so we can make a break for it.

We're almost at the door when I hear someone calling.

"Marsh." The voice is high and grating. It only takes me a second to place it. Logan, of course. I don't know why I'm surprised.

20
Confrontations

I pretend I don't hear her. Maddie and I are only a few feet away from the exit. *We can make it,* I think. *We can make it.*

But Logan's calling again, closer now. Against my better judgment, I turn, and there she is, elbowing her way through the mob. I almost groan out loud. Nothing good can come from this.

"Marsh," she says.

"Uh. Hey," I say.

Logan flashes her perfect teeth, glances at Maddie, and then shifts her eyes like it's just the two of us talking. "I didn't see you here," she says. "What's up?"

"*Pulse Referendum,*" I say.

"Yeah, I know. It was awesome." She sneaks another look at Maddie. "So, what are you doing here? Wow, when's the last time you were at a movie?"

My jaw drops. Is she freaking kidding?

More flashing of teeth. More breathy high voice. "Everyone's going over to Cup o'cino's now. Are you coming?"

The top of my throat starts burning just thinking about it. "Not today," I say, "but, hey, thanks for asking."

Logan smiles a pursed-lip smile. I'm thinking, *Whew, that's over,* but the next thing I know she's in my face. "So this is it? We're really over?"

"Uh . . . uh," I say, because the crowd's pushing at us from every angle. Strands of conversations flick at me—people reliving the great moments of the movie or calling out who's driving whoever to Cup o'cino's. When I catch Brad charging out of the restroom, I squeeze Maddie's hand without thinking about it.

"I can't believe this," Logan cries. "You're *with* her?" Her voice shrills out above the surrounding chatter. "Are you with her?"

Jeez. Are we going to do this now? I start to formulate possible answers—yes, no, I don't freaking know, and anyway, who are you to talk, Logan? Aren't you here with Brad?—but I can't settle on one; so instead, I just stutter like an idiot for a minute until Maddie drops my hand. She edges away from me, crosses her arms in front of her chest.

"We're just friends," she drawls, which somehow enrages Logan more.

"What do *you* know?" she screeches. "You just moved here. What, like, two weeks ago? You don't know Marsh. So just shut the hell up. Okay? Y'ALL."

I don't think it's the correct usage of the term, and I feel like pointing it out to Logan and while I'm at it, telling her to quit mocking Maddie about her accent too. "Look," I start to say, but damn it all to hell if the crowd's not parting so Brad can plow through.

"What's going on?" he demands. His bulbous lips flop out, all blotched gray and blue. And I notice one of his eyes is still marked up in matching gruesome colors.

I figure Brad's primed to defend Logan—his movie date, apparently—but he surprises me by pointing a stubby finger at Maddie. "Oh, man, Marsh," he says. "You must have a death wish." He jerks his head around. "Sam," he bellows. "Get over here."

I feel like I'm acting a part in a demented drama when Sam makes his entrance, stage left, his face throbbing tomato-red.

I curl my hands into fists. *Here we go again*, I think, but for some reason I'm not too freaked out about it. Maybe because I've acted in this play before. I know the script, my lines, and the stage directions. Scene Three: They fight. I can handle that role.

Sam pushes into our little circle, wedges himself between Maddie and me. She and Logan both shrink back, their faces frozen with the same expression. Fear, it looks like—for me and for whatever Sam's about to do, with Brad as his willing accomplice, no doubt.

Sam's arm is in slow motion when it whirls in an arc through the air. I raise my fists just as his arm hooks around my shoulder, tugging me closer.

"Let's talk," he spits in my ear, and I feel myself drifting away from Maddie and Logan and into the throng of people who press toward us, eager to see probable bloodshed in the middle of the theater lobby.

He backs me against a wall, his arm weighing me down. He's got one vein on his forehead that looks like it wants to punch out of his skin. "Maybe I haven't been clear," is how he starts off. "I don't know what you think you know about my sister, what you've heard about her," he says, "but whatever it is, you need to back off."

Okay. No idea what the hell the guy's talking about. I grab his arm, heave it off, and say my line: "No. *You* need to back off."

Sam takes a step backward. "I don't want to fight you."

The truth is I don't want to fight him either, but somehow I find myself leaning closer. The next thing I know, I'm crouched down like I'm on the football field. What I used to do during those one-on-ones with Chuck is swing my head to the left, so it looked like I was going to spring out that way, but then I'd pull back at the last second and drive forward right.

Without even thinking about it, I feel my head dipping, and as I do that, I'm flashed back to those football plays, where the field freezes at the whistle. But this time it's the theater lobby that's slowing down. I can scan the whole place at once—Sam facing me, tensing for my attack. Brad beside him, his multicolored lips puckered out.

And now I see Chuck too, shoving himself onto our stage. He's seen me, and his body bends, mirroring my own.

I suck in my breath, start my charge in the other direction, but before I can complete the hit, I see Maddie. She's wide-eyed, squeezing her way through the crowd so she emerges at Sam's side, right where I'm gearing up to slam into him.

"Marsh," she says, and just like that, I'm pulled back to myself, anchored into the moment—a moment, I'm not too happy to inhabit, truth be told. What the hell am I doing? I don't want to fight her brother.

I drop my hands, straighten up, try to breathe out some of my adrenaline.

"Madison," Sam says, "stay out of this. It has nothing to do with you."

Which strikes me as funny. I can't help it; I start laughing. They both shoot me a puzzled look before turning back to glare at each other.

"This is stupid," Maddie says, her voice shaking. "You can't keep doing this. It's not your job."

Sam rocks back and forth, his fisted hands digging into his sides like's he's fighting with himself too. "Someone has to, Madison, or you're going to be right back where you started."

Maddie flinches like he's slapped her.

I have to tense my shoulders, hold myself against the wall to keep from dropping into my attack position again. "Hey," I say, "why do you keep calling her that?"

He looks at me like he's forgotten I'm here. "What?"

"Madison. She doesn't like it. She wants people to call her Maddie."

Sam's eyes narrow into slits. "This is none of your business. *Madison* is none of your business. Get it?"

"Sam," Maddie says, "I told you. I can make my own decisions. I can hang around with anyone I want to hang around with."

"No. I'm telling you. This guy, this guy—you don't know what he thinks about you—how he sees—"

"Sam, please," Maddie says. She's crying. Crying. And the sound of it freaking tears at me.

"Leave her alone." The words heave out when I lean forward, drop my head to the left, drive toward Sam.

He grunts and topples backward. He's got his mouth open as I pound my fist into his jaw. Only one part of me catches Maddie whirling away, escaping into the crowd. But that thought—that Maddie's hurt, that she's still crying, that she's running away alone—that thought flits away when I turn back to beat her brother's face.

The scene plays out according to a script I haven't read, but somehow it all seems familiar. The theater security guys swoop toward us, barking out warnings that we need to exit the building. I feel fingers digging into my arm. It's Chuck pulling me off Sam, towing me through the lobby. He's gripping me hard, but I don't bother to shrug him off. I know he doesn't know his own strength sometimes. Anyway, I just want to get the hell out of here, and he's going to make sure that happens.

He hauls me out onto the sidewalk, jerks me past the theater, away from the surging audience. "Holy shit," he says, panting. "What just happened in there?" He loosens his hold but keeps a grip on my shoulder as he drags me farther away. "Marsh, man. What's with you?"

There truly is no good answer to this question. Nothing's going to come out of my mouth anyway. I can't catch my breath. We're halfway down Main Street and I have to stop, hunch over, brace myself. When I clutch my knees, pain surges through my knuckles.

I hurt Sam. Half of me wants to barge back into the theater and go at him again.

Chuck whacks my shoulder. He bends down across from me and we lock eyes like we're gearing up for a play. His face is white, glowing under the streetlights. He's staring at me like he's never seen me before.

And isn't that the truth? Anger courses through me. I could do it. I could slam into Chuck right now. Just like old times. Bash into his chest, lift his feet off the ground, hurl him backward. What would his face look like then, when I pin him to the sidewalk?

"Marsh?" Chuck says. He's still eyeing me, shaking his head. "Come on, man. I know we haven't been . . . uh . . . hanging out lately, but you want to give me a clue what's going on?"

My head's throbbing with what I want to say. But when the words surge into my throat, I feel like I'm choking on them. "No," is all I can gasp out.

Chuck jabs my arm. I feel his eyes still scanning me.

I look past him at the sky. It's darkening up, gray going to purple like the bruises on Brad's face. And soon, Sam's. And where's Maddie? I double over and Chuck whacks my back.

"Maddie," I croak out, and Chuck gives me another smack.

"Don't worry. I saw her taking off with those sophomore girls, Heather and Someone? Man." He barks out a laugh. "You trying to start some football-lacrosse war or something?"

I laugh too, even though it hurts my chest. We shuffle together toward Chuck's car, still heaving laughs.

It's not until Chuck turns down my street and we roll past Mrs. Hansel's house that I remember Maddie again, crying after the crap Sam said, whatever the hell he was talking about. Then I'm back to being pissed off and wishing he were here next to me, in Chuck's car, so I could punch him in the mouth again.

21
Visitor

My mother's clanking around in the kitchen. "Is that you, Marsh?" she says.

I grunt, race upstairs, and lock myself in the bathroom. I grip the sink when I take a look at my face in the mirror. It's not a pretty sight: fresh bruising around one eye; my nose, basically intact for a change but blood streaking out of my nostrils.

I'm panting again. My mind's still clogged up with the fight. I can't push it away.

I liked it. Hitting Sam. I don't know why. It's not me. I'm not a fighter. Times my brother and I used to go at it, it was never more than play fighting, fooling around. A release of energy. Something to do when you're bored. Like we'd be sitting in the den watching TV and one of us would jump up, start punching. But we were kids. You grow up. You learn that you're supposed to let your aggression out in sports. Not on someone's face.

If Chuck hadn't pulled me off, I could've kept going. I would've. I picture that for a few minutes: me slamming Sam. His face swims in front of me. My hand blurs, striking him again and again until he's just pieces of eyes, nose, lips. And then it's *my* eyes, nose, lips that I'm bashing in.

My stomach lurches. When I clutch it, my knuckles flame up.

"Marsh," my mother says. It sounds like she's right outside the door.

I have no idea what I'm supposed to say. I don't know this script. I don't know my character.

"Marsh," she says again. "Dinner's ready."

I clear my throat. "Be down in a minute."

The washcloth burns my skin. One eye is swollen shut and plumped out like an egg. I'm not going to be able to hide this.

When I head downstairs, I pass my old room. My mother's been on a cleaning rampage. My lone uninjured eye takes it in. No more stuff from the memorial site. The boxes from the other day are gone. She stripped the sheets off the damn bed too. What the hell?

"Oh!" my mother gasps, as soon as I burst into the dining room. "What happened to your face?"

I ignore that question. "Where'd you put those boxes?"

My father bangs his glass against the table. "Don't you dare talk to your mother like that."

I ignore that too. "Where?"

"The basement," my mother stutters. "Marsh, what happened?" She stands up, reaches her arms out.

But I shrug her away. "You were going to wait, you said. You were going to let me go through it first."

"Marshall," my father says, standing now too. "Did you get in another fight?"

My mother's crying. It's a quiet sob, where tears roll down her face and her shoulders heave up and down, but no noise comes out. What's wrong with me? I've hurt my mother yet again and all I can think about is the way she's crying.

I stumble out of the room, throw open the basement door. It's musty, murky in the back corner where my mother's stacked the boxes. I yank one of them down, tug at the flaps. She's got them taped up, like she wants to pack this stuff away for good. I can't get my fingers under the tape. I slap the top of the box, tear at the cardboard. My knuckles ache, but I don't stop.

I was always the one who quit first. That time we were locked out of the house—it was last winter, now that I think about it—I huddled on the back porch and braced myself, resigned to wait it out in the cold.

My brother, though, he wasn't the type of guy who took a locked door for something that'd keep you out. I watched him kick at the latch, his boot swinging out again and again, until he broke through, tore open the metal door, swung himself down into the basement. He was grinning the whole time too, when I followed him inside.

I've clawed open the box, plunged my hands into it. It's just junk left at the accident scene. Why does it mean anything to me? I pull out a deflated football, cradle it against my chest.

I don't know how long I sit there, my back pressed against the boxes. At some point, I stand up, flex the soreness out of my legs, chuck the football across the room.

Somehow I've forgotten my battered face, but that reality comes back to me when a burst of pain shoots across my eyeball. I head upstairs in search of an icepack, even though it's probably too late to counteract the swelling. I settle for a package of frozen peas. My good eye spies a plate of cold food left out on the kitchen counter. A hunk of steak, potato wedges, congealing corn; fork, knife, and spoon lined up on a nice little folded up napkin. My mother never quits either.

Unless you count boxing up mementos.

I carry my dinner upstairs, sprawl out across my brother's neatly made bed. While I chew my cold food, I keep my head tilted, the peas balancing on my eye, blink the other eyeball at the ceiling. The rocket ship on the poster never stops blasting off. Smoke never stops swirling out of the back end. I try to lose myself in the gray mist, but I can't.

A thought nags at me: Is it quitting to *stop* looking for a thin space? Or is it quitting to *keep believing* you'll find one?

At first I don't know where I am or what time it is. Someone's tapping on my door. Loud. Louder. My mother pokes her head in.

"Marsh," she whispers.

I shift around on the bed, hear a fork plink on the floor.

"Someone's downstairs to see you."

I try to blink, but only one eye moves, and I let out a groan.

"A girl," my mother says. "Maddie Rogers? She says it's important." She switches on the light, muffles a gasp. I can only guess what my face looks like now.

"Maddie?" I say. I squint at my brother's alarm clock. Almost nine o'clock.

"It's getting late. Do you want me to tell her you're sleeping?"

I grunt out a laugh. "I'm not sleeping." I heave out of the bed and realize I'm still holding a bag of peas, now thawed, in my hand.

"Marsh," my mother says. She reaches for me but then pulls her hand back. "I'm sorry. About before. About packing up—"

"It's okay." I wave, get a flash of my bruised knuckles clutching the wet bag. "Tell her I'll be right down."

First though, I have to change out of my reeking shirt. It's dusty from the basement and spattered with dried blood— mine or Sam's, it's hard to say. I grope under the bed, find my brother's slippers, stuff my feet into them. I don't bother to check my face in a mirror. Somehow I don't think a clean shirt's going to do much to help my appearance.

My mother's left Maddie sitting in the living room. When I get downstairs, all I see are her shoulders hunched over. She's practically swallowed up in our overstuffed couch.

"Your father and I are in the den watching TV," my mother whispers, retreating down the hall, and Maddie jerks her head up.

"Oh," is the first thing she says. It sounds like the beginning of a moan.

I brace myself in the doorway. "Maddie," I start. I'm fumbling around for an explanation here, something along the lines of me being an idiot for beating up her brother, but before I can plunge into it, she stops me.

"I didn't know where else to go," she says. "I had to get out. I couldn't stay there." She has her knees pulled up to her chest, and she wraps her arms around them, rocking back and forth, shuddering out sobs.

She's breaking down, it looks like, but I don't know what I'm supposed to do about it. "Did Sam, did he say—?" I sputter for a few seconds because I can't imagine anything Sam could say that would make Maddie freak out like this. It's like she's in shock or something. I'm finally unglued from the doorway, and I move toward her, kneel down in front of the couch. "Please, Maddie, tell me. What the hell happened?"

"I had to get out." She says it again, still shaking.

I squint my lone working eyeball in the direction of the den. Not that I'm thrilled about seeing my parents right now, but maybe this situation is beyond what I can handle. "Maddie, you're, uh, kind of scaring me here." I reach one of my bruised hands out and carefully as possible, for both our sakes, I touch her knee. "What's going on?"

She lifts her head and her eyes widen. "Mrs. Golden."

Okay, I didn't see that one coming. "Mrs. Golden?"

"My room . . . she's in my room." She goes back to rocking again, sobbing. Now I notice that she's wearing slippers and dressed only in sweats. Her hair's out of its usual ponytail and spilling around her shoulders.

I grab an afghan off the back of the couch, drape it over her, even though it's pretty warm in here. Then I perch next to her on the couch and pat her shoulder, because what else am I going to do?

She keeps crying. I keep patting her shoulder. I'm a little tense thinking one of my parents is going to pop in, wonder why the hell there's a girl having a nervous breakdown in the living room. They've got to know something's up, but for the time being maybe they want to avoid a confrontation.

Finally, it seems like Maddie's winding down. She lets out a few more sobby breaths, tightens her arms around her knees. "It's in my bedroom," she says, and her trembling voice makes my stomach coil up. "The thin space."

"What?"

"It's in my room!" she wails. "All this time we've been look-ing in the wrong place. And I've been sleeping in there. Those nightmares . . ." She stands and the blanket slips to the floor. "They were real. Those were real dead people coming through."

"Maddie." I shake my head because her words are tripping over each other. "Slow down. You're not making any sense."

She juts out her chin. "Mrs. Golden was in my room. I caught her sitting on my bed."

"Mrs. Golden?" I'm still not following the logic of this conversation. "Why would she be in your room?"

She sinks back down next to me. "I was home, alone. Sam never came back after the movies. He texted he was at Brad's, getting cleaned up. I guess his face is . . . kind of a mess too . . ."

"I'm sorry about that," I say, but she waves her hand.

"We forgot our mom wasn't going to be home anyway. She has a date tonight, some guy she met online, I don't know, whatever. She's still out with him."

I keep blinking one eye. "Mrs. Golden," I remind her. "I don't understand how—"

"She came over with more food, a plate of oatmeal cookies this time. I was so upset after the movies . . . I just wanted her to go away, but she kind of barged in with her cookies and sat down in the front room. I was thinking, okay, I guess she wants to visit with me, so I told her I'd get her a glass of milk, and she said a cup of tea would be better."

"Maddie," I say, because my head is spinning.

"I'm getting there," she snaps. "So I made her tea, and when I carried the cup into the front room, she was gone."

"Gone?"

"Right," she draws out the word. "I thought she left, went home. And I was thinking, oh well, she's kind of weird. I put the tea away and went upstairs to bed. It's so cold up there. You remember me saying that?"

I nod. Stuff is churning in my mind now, but none of it's fitting together.

"My room's the coldest room in the house." She shivers, grips her knees. "But I was tired. I just wanted to go to sleep. This day's been so long . . ."

True, I realize. Hard to believe it all started with Maddie and me sliding around the hospital, and that was before we even ended up at the movie theater and I spilled my guts out

200

to her, and then Logan and Sam and Chuck and—my head aches just thinking about it.

"But she hadn't left. When I went up to my room, I found her."

"Mrs. Golden?"

She shudders. "Yeah. She was sitting at the foot of my bed. With her back to me. Her whole body was shaking. I don't know what I was thinking, that she was having a seizure or something, but when I stepped closer, I saw—"

"What?" I say, because I'm trying to picture it: Mrs. Golden at the edge of a bed, her yellow poufed-out hair, her eyes glazed behind her glasses.

"Her shoes," Maddie whispers. "She had them on her lap. When I looked down, I saw that she had her bare feet on the floor."

—⁓⁓—

I grab two coats from the front closet, drape one around Maddie, yell down the hall to my parents. "I'm walking Maddie home. I might stay over there for a while."

"It's a school night," I hear my mother say, but we're out the door, tearing down the street.

It hits me that I'm still wearing my brother's slippers. Maddie's got slippers on too, and we skim along the icy sidewalk, clinging to each other, trying to keep from falling. The neighborhood's quiet, cold. Some of the houses are already dark, even though it's barely ten o'clock. Lots of old people around here. They turn in early.

"Do you think she's still up there?" Maddie says.

"If she is, we'll tell her it's time to go home." I feel my face twisting into a smile. Isn't that what Mrs. Golden told me once? *Marsh Windsor, time to go home.* And who's the crazy one now?

Mrs. Golden. Pushing her way into the house, welcoming Maddie's family with pies, but really she wanted to sneak away, take off her shoes—

But this doesn't make sense.

"Wait a minute." We stop in Maddie's driveway, and I squint one eyeball at the dark house. "How does Mrs. Golden know about thin spaces? Why would she even believe in something like that?"

Maddie snorts. "Something crazy, you mean?"

Good point. It is crazy. It's always been crazy. And yet—

"Her husband," Maddie says, "the one who died shoveling or whatever. Maybe she misses him, like desperately misses him."

I shrug, tap my slippers on the icy asphalt. "I don't know. He died a long time ago. God. I was in middle school. Would you still miss someone from that long ago? I mean when do you get over—?" But forget that line of questioning. It's too disturbing to contemplate. "Wait," I say again. "Let me think this through." I shift through my memory frame by frame. I picture the bed positioned in front of the fireplace. Mrs. Hansel, thin and pale, raising her hand.

The memory clicks and there's Mrs. Golden next to the bed, telling me I'm tiring Mrs. Hansel out. "She was there the last time I saw Mrs. Hansel," I say. "She would've overheard Mrs. Hansel talking to me. If she missed her husband, like you say, it could've gotten her thinking . . ." Maddie's shivering, nodding along, but there's still a piece of this that doesn't fit. "Mrs. Hansel died downstairs in the front room, that's where she had the hospice people set up her bed. How could there be a thin space in your bedroom?"

"I don't know." Her teeth are chattering. "Mrs. Golden was sitting on my bed. The way she looked, Marsh—with her shoes on her lap—I just had to get out of there."

"Okay, okay," I say. I try to keep my voice steady because Maddie's on the verge of losing it again.

The answer is so clear and yet impossible at the same time. That somehow Mrs. Hansel figured out she'd come through upstairs. That somehow, sick as she was, she managed to get up there. My head's pulsing so hard I feel like it's going to explode. I have a flash of Mrs. Golden bringing over cake and plants, cozying up to Maddie's family. She was trying to get into the house just like I was.

I slide toward the front door, forgetting Maddie for a second until I feel a squeeze on my arm. I look down and she's trembling.

"I can't stop thinking about my nightmares," she says. "Those people. Do you think they're real? Ghosts or dead people coming through the thin space? Coming into my room and standing at the edge of my bed—"

"Shh," I say, wrapping my arms around her shoulders, pulling her toward me.

"I'm scared." I can feel her breath against my neck.

"It's okay. I'll go up to your room. I'll check to see if she's still there."

I don't say the next part. I wonder if Maddie can feel that I'm shaking too.

Is this finally happening? After two months of searching, am I going to step into a thin space? Find my brother?

22
Hiding

Maddie tugs me back before I can make it past the third
stair. "No," she whispers. "I'm going with you."

"I thought you were afraid."

"You'll be with me." She takes my hand, joins me on the
stairs, but I stop.

"What?" she says.

I don't know how to say this. I've told Maddie more things
about myself than I've told anyone. In some ways, she knows
more about me than anyone alive in the world. But in another
way, she's just like everyone else. She knows nothing.

What I have to do in the thin space—and my heart stutters just thinking that it's possible after all—I've got to do it
alone.

"You can't go with me," I tell her. I keep my one eye looking
somewhere over her head, but I can feel her tensing beside me.

"Why not?" She squeezes my hand. "Marsh," she says, and
as always, my stomach clenches. "I told you about my father.

I know you want to see your brother. Can't we both go in together? See who we want to see and then come back out?"

I twist her hand away, turn, take another step up the stairs. When was the last time I was on these stairs? All those Saturdays helping Mrs. Hansel, lugging boxes down. How many times did I pass my brother here? We'd grin, groan. Those first few weeks when we hardly knew Mrs. Hansel and she was just the crazy widow, and we were ticking off service hours. And later, when we did know her—funny thing, even during football season, Mrs. Hansel could tell my brother and me apart.

"Marsh." Maddie's right beside me, tilting her head. "Answer me. Why not? We'll hold hands, take off our shoes. Our slippers, I mean, and we'll go in together, like we planned before."

I don't tell her that I have never planned to do it that way.

"Maybe we can see Mrs. Hansel too. Oh!" She waves her arms. "Do you think she's the lady, the one I saw at the edge of my bed?"

"Did she have white hair?"

She nods, her eyes wide.

We're at the top of the stairs now. There's a landing up here with four doorways. All the doors are open, and from where I'm standing, I can see into each room.

On my left, the pink-tiled bathroom. Next to that, Mrs. Hansel's sewing room, now clearly Sam's room, with his unmade bed pushed against the wall. On my right, Maddie's mother's room is a mess of clothes and shoes. When it was Mrs. Hansel's guest room, my brother was in charge of it, which was a job in and of itself—seventy-five years of storage, basically.

And straight ahead, Maddie's room—only a couple months ago, Mrs. Hansel's. It's the one room I never entered all those Saturdays. Mrs. Hansel kept the door closed, said it was too messy even for us to deal with.

Here on the landing, three feet from the doorway, I can already feel the chill. I step closer, reach up, drag a finger along the top of the doorframe. But there's nothing but dust.

"What are you doing?" Maddie whispers.

"Looking for, uh, stones."

She frowns. "To see if she was marking the room? Like the druids used to?"

I swipe my finger off on my jeans, nod. Did Mrs. Hansel really make a thin space here? I peer into the room. The bed's draped with blankets, different colored ones, a quilt, a sleeping bag unzipped and spread out on top of the pile.

"Is she still in there?" Maddie says softly.

For a second I think she means Mrs. Hansel. "No," I tell her, and mist swirls out of my mouth. "Mrs. Golden's gone."

I step over the threshold. Maddie's behind me, bumping against my back.

"It's so cold," she says. "Every night I wear socks to bed. Do you think that's why I never stepped through before?"

"I, uh, maybe, that's—" I can barely frame a coherent thought. I'm staring at the edge of Maddie's bed, where Mrs. Golden sat not too long ago, her bare feet pressed to the floor. What happened to her? Is she in the thin space?

"Where was she exactly?" I say. "Show me."

207

Maddie hesitates, then inches closer, marks out the area with a shaky finger. She holds her body rigid, away from it, trying to keep a distance. "Her shoes aren't here," she whispers. "Do you think that means she put them back on and went home?"

I shrug. Who the hell knows? The whole concept is nuts. I take two strides forward, and I'm standing right on the spot.

Maddie cries out.

But nothing happened, of course, because I'm wearing slippers. I wanted to touch it—the space—to see if it's different in any way from the surrounding area. I turn my head, squint my eye at Maddie. "It's colder here. You can feel it."

I wave my hands toward the ceiling, then squat down and tap the floorboards. I don't know what I expected. Except for the fact that it is noticeably colder, there is nothing that defines this space. No boundary. No curtain. No doorway. But somehow Mrs. Hansel knew that she came into the world here, knew if she wanted to make a thin space, she would have to drag her dying body up here too.

It's time now.

Time for me to go through. To do what I need to do. To fix what I set in motion last summer. I know it, but I can't make myself move faster. I'm in slow motion, pulling off my right slipper. It's my brother's, which somehow seems fitting.

"Marsh." Maddie touches my arm as I bend down, reaching for his other slipper. "Are you okay?" Her hair swirls around her shoulders. Her cheeks flush so pink.

My thoughts rush together, tumbling onto each other so nothing makes sense. *I'm almost in the thin space. I can find him. I can do this. I can fix this*—but running alongside that train is something else. It's one word—*Maddie*—over and over.

She's got her hands holding both of mine, anchoring me here at the foot of the bed. A part of me feels her grip, the pain shooting through my sore knuckles.

I can find him I can do this I can fix—
Maddie Maddie Maddie

"Are you okay?"

I don't know the answer. The truth is—"Maddie." And for some reason I hear myself blurting it out. "I want to stay here. I do. But I have to try this." I look at my brother's slipper on the bed. It's wet, I notice, from running down the street. I've probably ruined these slippers. Me, always the messy twin. I let out a strangled laugh. "You want to hear something funny?"

Maddie's forehead wrinkles up.

I can't stop myself. "Mrs. Hansel never mixed us up. My brother and me. When she called one of us, she didn't pause, she didn't have to look hard, she'd just say *Austin*, or whatever, *can you help me with this?* Other people, they messed us up all the time. That's why it was so easy to switch places. They didn't really look at us. They didn't really know us. And the girls. Logan and Kate. They were just like everyone else."

Maddie nods, but I know she doesn't get why I'm telling her this.

Truth. It's surging out of me. I'm opening up, expressing myself, letting it all out. Too bad I'm never going to see my doofball therapist again. If I did, I'd tell him: *You're right. It does feel good.* I let out another laugh, even though what I'm trying to say is so pathetic.

"I hated being a twin." I wait for Maddie's expression to turn to disgust, but there's nothing but a raised eyebrow. "I loved my brother, but one time I wished—well, we got into a fight, not a fistfight like I've been doing lately, but an argument. And I had this thought. It was so fast, Maddie. It went through my mind for one second—" I let out my breath, watch a wisp of mist roll out of my mouth. "I wished I wasn't a twin. That one second I wished I was just one person. Me. Alone." I feel myself sagging onto the bed, one bare foot pressed against the floor.

Maddie's arm's around my shoulders now. "Is that what you feel bad about?" she says. "You wished you didn't have a twin, and now you feel like it's your fault or something that he died?"

"Yeah." She presses closer. I could do it. I could tell her the rest. I pick the slipper up off the bed. I cradle it in my hands. "This is his, you know. My brother's. I'm going to leave it here and maybe he can . . . find it later."

Her eyes are searching my face. They widen and she snatches the slipper away from me. "Oh my God! I know what you're doing. You want to switch places with him. That's what you're doing. You don't want to see your brother in the thin space. You want to take his place in there. You want to—"

"Yes." The word rasps out of me, but the real word—*die*—hangs there too. Some kind of weight has been loosened. My whole body shudders.

Maddie and I stare at each other, our breath puffing out between us.

I'm emptied out. There's more to say and I should probably say it. Leave the world with a clear conscience.

"Marsh?" she says.

My stomach tightens up and I know I won't do it. I like Maddie, of course, but how can that change reality? "Let's go." I reach down to remove the other slipper.

"Wait." She jerks her head toward the doorway. "Do you hear that? A car." She springs up, tugs me away from the bed before I can think to stop her. "It's Sam," she says. "He can't see you in my room. You've got to get out of here."

"Hold on," I tell her. I clutch the doorframe, look over my shoulder toward the thin space. "He won't see me. I'm going in. I'm leaving. I'll—"

But she yanks my sleeve. "No. Not now. Please, don't do this." She tows me toward the stairs, and I don't know why I follow her. We hear a key clicking in the front door, and we're skidding down the hallway toward the kitchen.

"Maddie, I've got to—"

She flings the basement door open, shoves me down a step, tucks the slipper into my hand. "Please, Marsh." Then the door's shut, and I'm standing in the dark swaying.

At the same moment, Sam's voice booms down the hall.

"Madison."

I lean my head against the door, stifle a groan. I am such an idiot. I was right there, one slipper off, standing in the freaking thin space, and now what the hell am I doing? Locked up in a basement—

"Who's coat is that?"

I hear Maddie, low and clear. She must be standing right on the other side of the door. "No one's. Just, I borrowed it."

"Where's Mom?"

"On a date…"

"Ugh. Forgot about that."

I can hear the refrigerator opening. A drawer squeaking. Silverware rattling.

In a minute, Sam sounds like he's chewing cud. "What's wrong with you?"

"Nothing." Now Maddie's voice is farther away.

More loud eating. Sloshing of liquid.

I sink down, sit on the top stair, press my back against the door. There's just a slit of light slipping under. I can see three steps down. The rest of the basement is lost in the murk. Why does this feel so familiar?

I almost laugh. When was it? Two weeks ago? Is that possible? Could only that much time have passed since I was standing here, on this step, locked in this same dark basement?

Sam belches. "What's that?"

"My sleeping bag," Maddie answers. She sounds out of breath. She must've run upstairs and back down.

"I mean what're you doing with it?" Sam says.

"I'm sleeping on the couch tonight."

Another belch. "Why?"

There's a pause. The door shifts a little, so I know she's leaning against it again. "My room's too cold."

Grunt. "Whole house is cold."

"I'm not sleeping up there anymore."

"You can't sleep down here."

"Why not?"

"What about when she comes home?" he says, and his voice rises up high like I've never heard it before. "With the guy?"

"I don't care."

Dishes clatter in the sink. "Yeah. She's probably not coming home anyway. It's better," Sam says, "if she doesn't come home. My face like this." More grunting. "Brad shouldn't have pulled me off him."

I can see four steps down now. Maybe I should get out of here, use the other way out, sneak through the metal doors, go home. I imagine myself groping across the basement, hitting the back steps, leaping over the bucket of pebbles.

"The guy's messed up, Madison. You get that, right?"

The door creaks.

"You saw how he attacked me. I told him I didn't want to fight."

"He likes me," Maddie says in a small voice.

"*He likes me*," he mimics. "Don't kid yourself. He doesn't even know you."

"Yes, he does."

"Come *on*. Don't you realize how guys see a girl like that? Throwing yourself at them, like—"

"Like what?"

Long pause. "Nothing. Forget it."

"No. I get it." Her voice screeches into Logan territory. "You take that one time. One time. And you blow it all up just like everyone else."

"That's how it starts, Madison. What do you think? You go down a road and you can't get off it."

"It's not like that. I'm not doing that. It's different here."

"Right, Madison. That's what you want to tell yourself." Clomping footsteps across the linoleum. "Look in the mirror sometime. The truth is you're just like Mom."

I hear the clomping moving farther away, down the hall, up the stairs. When the steps shuffle overhead, the door opens and I stumble into the kitchen. I squint my eye, try to readjust to the light. Maddie's slouched in front of me. Her face is red, streaked with tears. Just seeing her like this makes me want to punch something.

"Messed up" is probably an accurate description of my state of mind. I'm wearing one slipper. The other one's clutched in my fist. I open my mouth but nothing comes out. I have no idea what my line is.

Maddie juts out her chin. "Come on," she says. "Let's get the hell out of here."

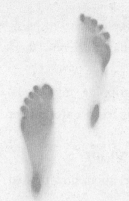

23
Thin Space

We tiptoe upstairs. Sam's door is closed, but I don't care about him. In two minutes, he's not my problem anymore.

The cold hits us a like a wall. Maddie closes her bedroom door behind us.

I drop the slipper on the bed, pull off the other one, and set that one down too. I hate to dump the issue of Sam on my brother, but I figure, what the hell, it's *his* turn now to deal with reality. I flex my feet, feel the cold wood floor. My breath's ragged when I cross the room.

"Wait," Maddie says.

"Maddie, no!" I practically wail. "I can't wait anymore."

She grabs my hands. I'm one foot away from stepping into the thin space, and she presses herself closer to me. "Just one minute, okay? I have to tell you something first."

I let out a sigh, but I can't help listening to her. She's so close to me. And it's nice, warm—someone holding me like this.

"They're things about me you don't know," she whispers.

I can't help laughing. "I got a news flash for you—there are things about me *you* don't know."

She pulls back, glaring but still gripping my hands. Probably she's making sure I'm not going to dart around her and disappear.

Okay, I can wait one more minute. "What?"

"You know the stuff I told you before, about how messed up things were after my father died?"

I nod. "Sam had to take care of you. Your mother remarried a couple of times."

"There's more. More . . . um . . . recent stuff."

"You can tell me," I say.

The color spreads across her cheeks. "I don't even know where to start. It's stupid. I wasn't thinking. Just, last year I went to a few parties. Lots of older guys went too, seniors, guys Sam hated. People drank, coupled up. Sometimes things got, I don't know, out of control. Once the police came. It was like this big scandal at our school. And Sam, he was so upset about it. Nothing really happened. I mean, I didn't really do anything. But he's just . . . crazy when it comes to stuff like that."

I don't think her face can get any redder than it is now.

"And then, at school people were saying stuff about me. It didn't matter what *I* said. To him. To them. This one stupid decision you make and you're branded for life. When we moved here, I thought maybe this was my chance. I could start over, be different, call myself Maddie, you know?" She heaves out a sigh. "But if Sam sees me that way, I mean, how do I ever get away from it?"

"Sam's wrong," I tell her, and somehow I'm holding her, whispering in her ear. "Maddie. I know who you are. Now. It doesn't matter what happened before. It doesn't matter what he thinks. It doesn't—" And then I don't know what comes over me, but I'm kissing her. Right here in the freezing cold room. It's crazy.

I'm crazy. What the hell am I doing? She's just told me a story about her supposedly bad reputation and now it's like I'm taking advantage of her—kissing her right after she's spilled her guts and feeling terrible about herself. I am such a complete ass.

"I'm sorry," I say, "I don't know why—"

But somehow we're kissing again. Nothing matters but this. I like kissing her. I like *her*. I don't know how it worked out this way or why. I don't care. The stuff she said, what Sam thinks, I don't give a crap about it. It's true what I told her. I know her now; that's the important thing here. I don't want to let go of her. I don't want to stop—

I've got to though. This is wrong. I'm leaving. In a minute, I'm disappearing into the thin space. All of this—whatever Maddie and I have—is over. I have to find my brother. I have to fix this mess. I made a mistake and I know it's the only way—

"You're still going through with it," Maddie says. She's rigid now in my arms.

"I have to." I know I am delaying the inevitable, but I kiss her one more time.

"Don't do this." She clutches my hand. "Please. At least let me go with you. Not to stay, like you—"

I'm shaking my head, but she keeps talking.

"I want to see my father. I want to see if he knows me. Me, who I really am, and not that person Sam is disgusted with."

"Maddie." I groan, kissing her once more.

"Please," she says. She kicks off her slippers.

Who knows what makes me say it? There is so much about myself that eludes me these days. "Okay." I squeeze her hand. "We'll go in together."

The moment slows, freezes, as we stand, shakily, at the edge of Maddie's bed. I stare at my foot as I nudge it forward. I feel Maddie tensing beside me. Her head bobs as she moves forward too, her fingers digging into my hand, and then my heart seems to jump into my throat. The room slides away.

It happens just like Mrs. Hansel described. The bedroom walls, the bed piled with blankets, the ceiling, the wooden floor—everything narrows, blurs, and in a whoosh we're rushing past all of it.

I can't get my bearings. There's no top or bottom. I can't even tell if I'm falling or rising. It's like being plunged into a deep pool, but I'm not wet. I can't see the surface or the bottom. I flail around, enveloped in cold.

At some point, I can't feel Maddie's hand anymore, and I cry out. She's lost. I'm lost. The air's black, thick, and I'm still tossing around in it. Where's the mist? This isn't how Mrs. Hansel explained it.

My chest squeezes. I open my mouth. I'm waving my arms. I can't breathe. I'm drowning in the thick cold.

"Mrs. Hansel." I hear the word, shaky and scared. "Mrs. Hansel!" It's my voice, I realize, and that scares me too, but then someone's touching my arm, and I'm no longer falling and flailing.

The dark leaks away. I'm standing on something solid. I can't see my feet through the mist. The surface is smooth, slippery as ice. Fog swirls around my body, gray and thick. When it pulls apart, Mrs. Hansel sways beside me.

She looks exactly the same as the last time I saw her—her white hair, her nightgown. All that's missing is the sickbed and the oversized pillow.

"You called me," she says.

"Mrs. Hansel. You—"

"I know." She smiles. "I've looked better."

That's kind of the understatement of the year. The truth is, she looks dead. Her skin's as gray as the fog. Her eyes are sunken. Her body's skeletal.

Her voice sounds chipper, though. "I misled you, I'm afraid." She wags a bony finger at me, and I try not to flinch. "You thought I died downstairs. But after you left, a strange impulse seized me. I felt compelled to go upstairs to my bedroom. How was I to manage it, though, when I could barely lift my head? Thank goodness dear Linda was there to help. She was here too, not long ago. We had a lovely chat before she went off to visit with her husband." She laughs lightly. "I was so muddled that day, I bungled everything up. I forgot to tell Linda about the bare feet. I forgot the stones. Not that I would've been able to line them up properly. I kept hoping you'd both figure it out. But you're a smart boy." She pinches my cheek with two sticklike fingers. "Oh my, you've hurt yourself. Have you been fighting?"

"Yeah—I—" I can't stop shivering. This place makes Maddie's bedroom seem like a sauna.

Mrs. Hansel seems to know what I'm thinking. "It's very cold. You won't be able to stay here long."

"Mrs. Hansel—" My mind's whirling. I can't tear my eye away from her—how terrible, how *deathly* she looks. I clutch at my stomach. I'm afraid I might be sick.

"I'm glad you came. I'm glad you called me," Mrs. Hansel says. "I always liked you. Such a sweet young man." She sighs, and her thin frame rattles.

She sways closer, hugs me against her. I don't want to offend her, but I'm afraid if I hug her back, I'll crush her. Of course, she's already dead. The thought flits through my head and I have to suck in my breath, try to steady myself. I realize that I might be on the verge of a mental collapse.

When she lets go, she seems upset. "Lately, dear, I've been disturbed by your behavior. You haven't done what you're supposed to do."

"I know, I—" My teeth won't stop chattering. My body won't stop shaking.

"You've been wasting time. Lying to everyone. Lying to yourself. And that's not the worst of it. You've been hurting him."

"Hurting—?"

"He doesn't want to *be* here anymore."

"I know—that's why I—see I'm going to—"

Mrs. Hansel glares at me. "Well, what are you waiting for?"

I blink my eye. She's right. What the hell am I doing? I'm here, in the thin space. I have to do what I've set out to do. "How?" My voice croaks out. "How do I find him?"

"You know."

It's so clear, so easy. When it hits me, I practically start crying. "Thank you," I tell her.

She hugs me again, pulls back, and smiles. The fog thickens around me until I can't see her anymore. I can't see my feet, my hands. I whirl in a circle, doing what I know I have to do.

I call him.

And just like that a dark figure rolls out of the mist.

I take in the dark hair, the black T-shirt, the jeans; he's limping, dragging his right leg through the gray toward me. Closer and I throw my hands up to my mouth. The accident shoots through my mind, my fists around the wheel, his body pitching forward, his head turned, cracking the windshield.

It's hard for me to look at him. He may as well just have staggered out of the wrecked car. One side of his face is blackened with blood. I can't find his right eye under the mass of bruising. The rest of his body's no better off. His right arm hangs loosely, awkwardly at his side.

I clear my throat, not that it does much good. My voice is hardly more than a squeak.

"Hey," I say. "Marsh."

"Austin," he says, and the left side of his mouth turns up into a half grin.

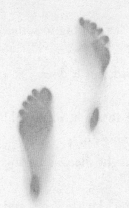

24
Brothers

"Austin," he says again.

And my body's like Jell-O. My legs buckle. My breath sputters out like I'm crying, laughing. I can't stop. It's seeing him. Hearing him. Hearing him say *my name*.

"So, I guess we were wrong about her being crazy," he says.

"Yeah. Ha ha. Uh. I'm sorry," I start babbling. "It took me so long to—I was trying to figure out how to come through. I've been working on it for a while and I—"

He lifts his left arm up. That side of his body seems to be working properly at least. "Relax, little brother," he says. "I know what you've been doing." He grins another half smile. "I've been coming through in Maddie's room."

"Maddie?" I whirl around. How could I have forgotten her? Where the hell is she?

Marsh seems to know what I'm thinking. "Don't worry," he says. His voice is calm, low. Hearing it gets me shaking harder. I haven't thought about this, how much I've missed hearing his voice. "Maddie's fine. I saw her talking to someone back there. Don't worry about her."

I don't know why this makes me mad, but it does. "You act like you know her."

He laughs. "Well, I've been coming through, like I told you. I've been keeping up with what's going on."

The idea makes me wince. "She thought she was having nightmares."

"That wasn't me. I never let her see me." He tries to shrug but only the left side of his body twitches up. "I know what I look like."

What am I supposed to say to that? The truth is he's a horror movie come to life.

"Anyway, I only did it a few times. I just wanted to see what you were up to. I stopped, though. I'm not like Mrs. Hansel. I'm not like these other ones." He drags his left arm through the mist.

"What do you mean?"

"I don't want to be here anymore." He flails his arm. "I mean, look at this place. I'm lost in a fog here."

I must be losing my mind because I start laughing.

He glares at me with his left eye.

"I'm sorry." I have to clutch my stomach. I really think I'm going to be sick. "I feel like I've been lost in a fog too."

"Yeah, well, that's your choice, Austin." He's still glaring. "Me? I'm stuck here. I'm lost, literally, in a freaking fog."

This is it, I realize. Time to fix this. Time to make this right. I straighten up, square my shoulders back. Now that I'm facing him, I don't know how we do it exactly, but I'm trusting that he'll know. "Okay," I say. "I'm here. You can go now."

His one eye rolls around. "Where am I going?"

"Back," I tell him. "I'm going to—"

He barks out a laugh. "I'm dead. You know that, right?"

"Yeah," I sputter, "but I was thinking we could—"

"Switch?" He hunches forward, clutches his left side, still laughing. "And how are we going to pull that one off, little bro?"

"I don't know." I'm getting angry again. I'm glad though. It's better than feeling like I'm going to vomit.

"It's not possible," he says.

"Why not? It's crazy what's going on right now." My voice sounds like it's rising toward hysteria and I have to take a breath so I don't keel over. "You . . . died in August and we're standing who the hell knows where having a conversation."

He shakes his head. "You're looking at me, right?"

Now it's my turn to roll my eye. "I've got injuries too," I tell him. "I got in a fight today."

"Someone punched you." He sneers. "My face smashed through a car windshield. It's not the same thing, I hate to tell you. Anyway, the real issue is that you're alive and I'm dead."

I'm full out crying now. Marsh pats my shoulder with his good hand. I don't care that he's gruesome—I love him. I hug him. I breathe him in. We haven't held each other in years, maybe never—I can't remember. But it feels right to be with him again, to not be alone. Stupid that that's what I wished for that one second—that I could be apart from him, be twinless.

225

"It's okay," he says, like he knows what I'm thinking. "It's okay."

I can't stop crying. He's dead.

Oh my God, Marsh is dead. Why is this such a shocking revelation? I've known he was dead since I woke up in the hospital.

"Wait," I say. I let go of him, step back a little into the mist. "You said you didn't want to be here anymore."

He nods, that smirky grin back on his face.

"So where do you want to go, then, if you don't want to switch places with me?"

A sigh hisses out of the side of his mouth. "I want to go on. Get it? I want to pass out of this place and die for real. Go on to the next world."

"Yeah, so why don't you do that?"

"Because of you."

"Me?"

"You're not letting me go."

I shake my head. I don't know what the hell he's talking about.

"The accident wasn't your fault," he says.

"You sound like Mrs. Golden."

"I'm telling you. It wasn't your fault. I know what you're thinking, but you're wrong."

My stomach won't stop lurching. "But it was my idea. I got us into this."

"Maybe, but it's not like you held a gun to my head. I went along with it."

I shake my head again, grip my stomach.

"Hey," he says, "when the hell have you ever been able to force me to do anything? Tell me that. Never. I was a willing participant. Yeah, it all turned out kind of shitty. But that's the way it is. It happened the way it happened, and it's not going to change. I died. You didn't. That's reality. The only thing left is for me to go on. And I can't do that until you do what you have to do."

"And what is that?" My voice chokes out, and next thing I know I'm bent over, heaving into the mist.

He pats my back while I'm sick. It takes a while before it's all out. It doesn't help that I'm crying like a blubbering idiot. It doesn't help that he keeps saying in his familiar, low voice, "It's okay, Austin. It's okay."

When I'm done, I drag my sleeve across my mouth.

"Feel better now?" he says softly.

What's the answer to this question? Marsh is dead. I'm alive.

"You know what you have to do now, right?"

I sway, dizzy. I do—God help me.

"Please," he says. "I'm counting on you." I scan him quickly, overlooking the gruesome parts, trying to hold on to what I want to remember of him. The eyes—like mine, I guess. The hair, short, nothing more than a buzz cut, like mine always used to be. The shoulders, broad and strong from football.

"Marsh." It's Maddie calling from somewhere out there in the mist. "Marsh."

My brother jerks his head toward the sound. "Go on," he says. "You can start by telling her."

227

25
Truth, Really

Maddie reaches for me in the fog. Her eyes are wild, wide. I pull her close to me, hide my face in her hair. I don't want her to see me like this. I'm a raw wound.

"I saw him," she says excitedly. "My father. Did you find Austin?"

I don't answer. My brother's broken body limps across my mind. *Tell her*, he says. Maddie and I slip along the icy surface. I wave my hand, trying to push the cold mist out of the way. *Tell her, tell her.* I wish I could make him stop. I wish I could push his voice away with a wave of my hand.

"How do we get out of here?" Maddie says, her teeth chattering.

"I don't know." Mrs. Hansel didn't mention this part, and I never asked her. Funny thing—I never planned to leave the thin space.

Around us, in the distance, dark shadows slither. Could we hide from them? Lose ourselves in the mist? Stay here forever?

Maddie shivers against me and gives me my answer. I have to get her out of here. I hold her tighter, rub my hands up and down her icy arms. "Look," I say. "Look for your bedroom."

The words are only halfway out of my mouth when the mist blurs, narrows, rushes away. It's the same as how we tumbled into this place, but this time I don't let go of Maddie. I clutch her to me as we fall and rise and whirl through the thick, cold blackness. I'm almost out of breath when Maddie's room slides back around us.

We find ourselves standing at the edge of her bed, still clinging to each other, both shivering, panting in her cold bedroom. Maddie has the same idea I do—quickly, we snatch our bare feet away from the floor, fall backward on the bed. I grope around for my brother's slippers and push them onto my feet.

Maddie grabs my arm. "Marsh, is that you?"

I suck in my breath like I've been punched. Because Maddie's squinting at me, frowning—

—pausing—

—trying to figure out who I am. She's wondering if my brother has taken my place.

I don't know if I can take this—*Maddie* squinting at me this way, *Maddie* not knowing for sure.

"Maddie," I say.

She smiles, presses her face against my chest. I can feel her sighing into me. She does know me. She does. I let out my breath. "Maddie," I say again, because I know I haven't answered her question.

I remember my brother's lost out there—dead—in the thin space, but somehow not dead too. And that part—that part out of everything truly is my fault.

"He's dead." My voice croaks out. "I'm alive."

"I know," she says. "I know, Marsh."

"No." I don't mean to say it so loudly. I put my hands around her face, make sure that she's really looking at me. *Tell her.* It is the only way to set him free. Maybe the only way to set me free too. "No." I say it softer this time. "Please don't say . . . Marsh anymore." I heave out a breath. "I'm not Marsh, Maddie. I'm Austin."

Her face is frozen in my hands. Her eyes aren't blinking. "Austin?"

I can't help shivering at the way the word comes out of her mouth. She is the second person to call me by my name today.

"Austin," she says again.

I feel like I'm hurtling through the air, but this time when I land, I'm falling into myself.

"What?" she says. "How did that . . . happen?"

My hands tremble against her face. I have to let go of her so I don't rattle the teeth out of her head. "We switched places, remember?"

Maddie nods. Her eyes are wide, her mouth, half open.

"My brilliant idea to see if Kate and Logan really knew us. Kate was *my* girlfriend, Maddie. Logan went out with Marsh. We dated those girls for like a year and a half, but Logan still thought I was him that day on the football field. They didn't really know us. That's why I talked Marsh into switching places. We wore each other's clothes. We traded wallets. Driver's licenses . . ." I tug his wallet out of my back pocket, flip it open, tap my brother's face. "That's him. That's Marsh." Why is the picture so blurry? Why can't I see it anymore?

Both of my eyes are leaking tears, even the one that's mostly swollen shut. *My brother's dead,* is what I'm thinking. Marsh *is dead.*

"I don't understand." Maddie's face swims in front of me. "Are you saying the accident happened the same night you switched places?"

I nod. "Bad timing, right?" I let out a strangled laugh. "Kate and Logan were clueless. The whole time Kate was pawing all over Marsh, and he let her. That's what pissed me off so much. Why'd he let her?" I close my eye, see the whole crappy scene at the movie theater again. "After we drove the girls home, he just laughed it off, said, 'Well that went well'—like it was no big deal. I wanted to punch him. I mean, I didn't kiss Logan."

I can't stop shivering and it's not just because I'm freezing. I have to wrap my arms around my stomach to try to keep myself from flying apart. "I asked him in the car. I said, 'Why the hell did you kiss Kate?' You know what he said?"

Maddie shakes her head.

"He said he didn't know. He didn't plan to. He was sorry. He said the same thing you did the day we went to that nursing home. We tricked them. It was wrong. We shouldn't have done it. He wasn't mad at the girls. 'It's just the way it is,' he said, 'being a twin. It's how it's always been.' Then he has the nerve to ask me when I'm going to get over it. I wanted to beat the shit out of him. He got pissed off, said it was my idea to switch in the first place. He told me to let him out of the car. He took his seatbelt off right before the other car swerved in front of us."

I don't know if Maddie can even understand what I'm saying because on top of crying, now my teeth are clacking together. "When I woke up in the hospital, I knew he was dead, but I didn't know at first they all thought it was *me*—Austin—who died. By the time I figured it out, it seemed like it was too late."

"Your parents," Maddie says, her forehead wrinkling up. "Why didn't they know? You said they could always tell you apart."

"They could. Before." I feel my shaky fists clench up and I focus on straightening out my hands. There's no point being mad at my mother and father. I can see that now. "But my face was so messed up and swollen. My forehead split apart on the steering wheel. My nose was broken. The people at the hospital told my parents that Austin died. And there I was, alive, and wearing Marsh's clothes. With his wallet in my pocket."

"But you," Maddie says. "Why didn't *you*—"

Of course this is the million dollar question. Why the hell didn't I tell anyone the truth?

"Maddie. I don't know." I think I might be sobbing. "I was so confused. In pain. Crazy, I guess, with grief. I started thinking it was my punishment. For talking Marsh into switching places. For hating being a twin. For wishing

I wasn't. Everyone thought Austin was dead, and I was thinking—well, yeah, I *am* dead, in a way."

I shove my hands under my legs to stop them flailing. "I was a mess for a few weeks. I couldn't even get out of bed. I've been sleeping in Marsh's room because I was supposed to be him. But that was a punishment for me too, to be surrounded by all his things. My parents tried to give me space. They wouldn't really look at me. Even when my face healed, they wouldn't really look at me. Nobody does, Maddie. Nobody ever looks at me."

"I look at you," Maddie says in a small voice. For some reason she's crying now, and I feel like I should comfort her, but when I lean closer to touch her, she shakes her head. "What about the thin space?" she says. "When did you start to look for it?"

"About a month after the accident I found out Mrs. Hansel was dying. I went to visit her that last time, and here's the craziest thing of all: she knew me. There she was, in her bed downstairs, one step away from death, but she looked right at me and called me Austin. No one had called me by name in weeks, and I practically fell over on the floor.

"Mrs. Golden was there, listening. She didn't catch what Mrs. Hansel said, or who knows, maybe she just thought Mrs. Hansel was confused, tired. She told me to leave, and I did, but I couldn't stop thinking about how Mrs. Hansel looked at me. Like she knew everything, and if I just listened to her, did what she said, all my problems would be solved. The second I walked out of the house, I took off my shoes. I thought it was the answer. I thought I could fix everything if I could find a thin space. I didn't want to switch places with my brother; I wanted to switch *back*. I wanted him to get to be Marsh again, and I wanted to die because everyone already believed Austin was dead anyway."

I have to stop here. I'm shivering so violently I'm afraid I might be sick again. I press a trembling hand against my mouth, take a few shallow breaths, and then manage a deeper one.

"Maddie," I stutter, afraid to look at her. "I'm sorry. I lied to you. I lied to—"

"Austin."

Oh God, I like hearing her say my name.

"It's okay," she says. It's the same thing Marsh just said to me.

It's a dumb phrase, really, when you think about it. In some ways it means nothing. Hearing Maddie say it now, though, I don't know. I can't help it. I choke out another sob. She hugs me. I guess she doesn't care what a mess I am, how I've practically just had a nervous breakdown in her bedroom.

"It's okay," she whispers again.

It reminds me of the story Mrs. Hansel told. How when she was a little girl she found a thin space in that abandoned old house. It's like what her father told her. Something occurs to me. I don't know what happened to Maddie out there. I want to hear it. I want to know.

"Maddie, did you see your father?"

I feel her shudder against me. "Yeah," she says. "He looked so sick. I was scared at first, but he kept smiling at me. It was so unbelievable to be with him again, to talk to him." She tilts her head back. "Thank you for letting me come with you. Thank you for everything, for telling me about the thin space, Mar—Austin." Her face flushes. "I'm sorry. I didn't mean to—"

"It's okay," I tell her. Because it is. Because it has to be.

I don't know how long we hold each other. I could stay here forever. I want to. Finally she lets go, stands up.

"It's getting late." She tugs my hands, leads me across the cold room. "Austin," she says.

"What?"

"I just wanted to say your name. Get used to it, you know?"

God help me if I start crying again. I suck in my breath, open the door, take a step into the hall, and find myself face to face with Sam.

26
Reality

He's holding his lacrosse stick, his black and blue face twisted with rage. "You? What the hell are you doing in my house, in my sister's room?"

Somehow I don't think he'll believe the truth. It doesn't matter. What he really wants to know is if I've hurt Maddie. "Sam," I say, keeping my voice steady. "Nothing happened. We were just—"

But he doesn't let me finish. He jabs the stick at me. I jump back but not far enough. It stabs my hip, the force of it knocking me into the wall. The stick pulls back, streaks toward me again.

Maybe there's a part of me that wants this to happen, that thinks I deserve this for all the pain I've put people through. Because I let him hit me twice more before I lunge forward, rip the thing out of his hands.

We're both breathing hard when Maddie pushes herself between us. "Stop," she says. "You can't do this, Sam. I told you. It's not your job. I can handle myself."

"Madison, listen," Sam starts to say, but Maddie cuts him off.

"No. You listen. Maybe I look like Mom, but I'm not her. And I know you want to protect me and I know how much you hate it. When she brings guys home. When she acts like she doesn't care about herself. But it's not me. Okay. It's not. And I'm sick of you—"

"Madison—"

"And don't call me that. I'm Maddie. That's my name. That's what Daddy used to call me."

"Daddy?" Sam says, in that strange high voice again. He leans against the wall, still trying to catch his breath. "What's he got to do—"

The front door bangs open. All three of us whip our heads in that direction. Not so funny thing, it's their mother whirling, laughing into the house.

"Oh!" Her voice echoes in the entryway. "Y'all are still up?" There's a man behind her, laughing too. "Tad." She giggles. "I mean Todd, these are my kids, Sam and Madison, and—" She takes a staggering step toward the stairs. "And some other boy I don't know. Hello there." She flutters her fingers toward me.

I'm afraid to look at Sam and Maddie. Their bright faces flash out of the corner of my eye.

"Tom," their mother's date grunts out.

"What? You know that boy?"

"No. *My* name is Tom."

Across from me, Sam sags against the wall. I can see we've got something in common, Sam and me. Besides the fact that we've both got bashed in faces, courtesy of each other, there's a part of us that halfway likes being hit with a stick, if only because it gives us a break from our secret pathetic realities.

Maybe Sam knows what I'm thinking. He grabs the lacrosse stick away from me, and I have a quick thought that I'll let him hit me with it again if he wants to. Instead, he throws an anguished look at Maddie, and then he stalks into his room and shuts the door.

I notice Maddie eyeing her bedroom. She's thinking about escaping too. Maybe she's imagining herself stepping back into the thin space and disappearing. I know that because I realize it's what I've been doing all this time, shuffling around barefoot instead of dealing with reality.

"It's going to be okay," I say to her. To myself. It's stupid, but it's the only thing that makes any sense. I take Maddie's hand, squeeze it, tug her away from the icy doorway.

We pass them on the stairs. Maddie's mother and her date are still whooping it up, laughing, as they stumble by us.

"Don't do anything I wouldn't do, sweetie," her mother slurs.

"Hey, what's wrong with that kid's face?" the guy says.

We can hear them groping around on the landing, her mother's shoes clicking against the hardwood floor.

When a door slams upstairs, Maddie shakes off my hand.

"I'm sorry," I say. I am full of clichés lately, but sometimes there's nothing else to fall back on. I hear a blur of voices in my head, the day I came back to school after the accident, all those meaningless platitudes. "I'm sorry," I say again.

There's a sleeping bag rolled out across the couch in the front room. Maddie sinks down on top of it. "I guess I'm going to sleep down here tonight," she says. "Maybe every night from now on."

I stride into the room, feeling the tilt of the floor as I walk toward the fireplace where Mrs. Hansel once lay, toward the couch where Maddie sits shivering.

"Your mother—"

But she holds her hand up. "I know."

I sit down next to her, start channeling Mrs. Golden and my doofball therapist, start telling Maddie that she's got to open up, express herself, let it all out.

She just says, "Austin."

Why does hearing my name make my heart swell up?

"Sam and I have lived with this for a long time," she says. "It's the way things are. We can't do anything about it. We can't change it."

What do I say to her? Something thumps upstairs and we both look at the ceiling. Maddie's face glows beside me. A part of me wants to lift her up, run her out the front door, take her away from here. Be like Sam, I guess, and try to protect her. Another part of me knows I can't do that, that it's her pathetic reality to deal with herself—that all I can do is be with her, squeeze her hand, whisper that it'll be okay.

So I do that for a while. We sit next to each other in the dark, slanted room. I hug her too. Because I want to. Because it keeps me here with her. For a few minutes, there is nothing else but this.

"Austin," she whispers, and I smile. "It's getting late."

I squint at the ceiling.

"Don't worry," she says. "I'll be all right."

"Are you sure?"

She pulls away, yawns. "This was a long day."

No kidding.

She leans back against the arm of the couch, tugs at the sleeping bag, yawns again. I start to lean toward her, but she presses her hand against my chest. "You should probably go."

"I don't want to."

She raises her eyebrow. "I know. But I just told Sam I could take care of myself."

"So you're kicking me out?"

She smiles, kisses my cheek quickly. "Thank you for telling me about your brother, what really happened."

I force myself to stand up. "Now I remember why I don't want to leave."

"Just so you know, I won't tell anyone. I know you'll tell people when you're ready."

When I'm ready. The phrase almost makes me laugh. When I'm ready.

The truth is, I'll never be ready. My parents. Kate. Logan. Chuck. The people at school. How do I tell them all?

But somehow I've told Maddie. And the world didn't split apart. I look at her now, the heart shape of her face, her hair flipping up around her shoulders. It's not fair really, that she likes me. That I like her. That I get to be here, alive, gazing at her, while my brother, Marsh—

I understand it now, why he's stuck in the thin space, how I've hurt him. It's not what I thought before—my stupid idea to switch places, my slow reflexes driving the car that night.

It's lying to everyone, like Mrs. Hansel said. It's lying to myself.

"Tomorrow," Maddie says. "We'll see each other tomorrow. Okay, Austin?" I lean down and kiss her forehead. I grab a blanket off the back of the couch, tuck it over the sleeping bag, because it's really cold in this room. Then I tell her goodbye and walk back up the slanted floor.

It's cold where my brother is too. And I can't make him wait anymore.

The street's dark, quiet, when I slip toward home. The snow's stopped. There's a full moon hole-punched in the black sky. I'm the only one out here, breathing mist in and out, pushing myself forward.

How many times have I shuffled back and forth on this sidewalk these past few months, barefoot, looking for a way out?

I've been an idiot. I know the answer. I've always known it. It's got nothing to do with taking off my shoes. It's got nothing to do with searching for doorways out of this world.

Tell, tell, tell, says my brother's low voice.

I smirk at the black sky. Easy for him to say. What the hell is going to happen when I do? When my parents find out they've buried the wrong son and etched the wrong name on his tombstone? When Logan learns that her boyfriend's been dead since August? When Kate finds out the love of her life has been alive all this time? When Chuck—

When Brad—

When Sam—
When Mrs. Golden—
When the doctors—
When my teachers—
When—
But now I've made it home.

My brother's dead. And I'm alive. This is the truth and I'm the only one who can tell it.

I open the door. I've got one foot in the house when I hear my mother's voice.

"Is that you, Marsh?"

I heave out a sigh. Steady myself. My face flashes back at me in the hallway mirror. I know my line of course.

"Marsh," she says again. "Is that you?"

There is so much I have to say, but I start by answering the question.

"No."

Acknowledgments

I love reading acknowledgment pages. For years when I was plodding along, figuring out how to break into print, I read the acknowledgments of my favorite books as a way to chart out who's who in the mysterious publishing industry and to get a glimpse into the lives of "real" writers. Now it's time for me to return the favor. It IS true what they say: no book is what it is without the help and support of a whole lot of people. Here are some of mine:

My awesome editor Gretchen Stelter, who nudged me along through an intense summer of rewrites. I bow down to you, Gretchen, for your editing skills but also because you are the only person I know who does aerial yoga.

All of the cool people at Beyond Words Publishing, especially Lindsay Brown and Emmalisa Sparrow, who read Marsh's story and loved it as much as I do. And a special shout out to my copy editor Linda Meyer, who was kind enough to point out my over-reliance on several particular words . . . "Jeez," as Marsh would say.

My first agent Mary Grey James, who plucked my manuscript out of the slush pile, and then when she retired, her partner, Deborah Warren, who picked up where MG left off. Deborah Vetter and Cicada Magazine for giving me my first shot. Sally Oddi at Cover to Cover Bookstore for passing along ARCs, talking books, and helping me plan a launch. Kim Griswell and Judy Burke and everyone at Highlights for making me believe I am a writer.

My mentors Marcia Thornton Jones and Tracy Barrett. All of my first readers, especially Jill Bixel, Sandra and Courtney Berger, Ella Koscher, Robin Gibson, Linda Eskildsen, Janet Buchas (love you, Auntie Jan!), and Pat Papagna (love you, Mom!). Anisha Andrews for sharing her identical twin experiences. Lisa Politz for being brutally honest and absurdly optimistic (so far you have always been right!). Jason Gobble, who has stuck his neck out for me on more than one occasion, and Tom Lamb, who has the distinction of having read EVERY SINGLE THING I've ever written since I was 18. I owe you guys. Big time. My chosen sister Deb Rogers for telling me two billion times: "This one is going to be the one." THE best writing friend and partner ever: Donna Koppelman. Your turn next, lady. (Also, you owe me a hair dryer.)

And last, but so not least, my ridiculously supportive husband and children. Rick, I don't deserve you. Ben, you are the smartest person I know. Brilliant Jane, who changed the course of this book with a simple question. Your name, sweetie, will be on a book one day too.

Discover more.

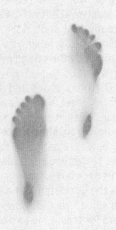